Draw YOU IN

USA TODAY BESTSELLING AUTHOR
MK MEREDITH

MK Meredith
P.O. Box 1724
Ashburn, VA 20146
Visit my website at www.mkmeredith.com.

Edited by Jessica Snyder and Jessica Wiers Serevino
Cover design by Kari March Designs

ISBN: 978-0-9990854-7-9
Manufactured in the United States of America
First Edition September 2018

PRAISE FOR DRAW YOU IN

INTRODUCTION

Hello!

I am so thrilled to share my happy ever afters with you, and I hope you love this book! If you haven't yet, enjoy your introduction to the wonderful town of Cape Van Buren with *One Jingle or Two* **FREE** on all e-retailers. Once you fall in love with Alora and Nate (they're irresistible, LOL!), you won't want to leave.

Which makes me so excited to offer you the opportunity to meet Blayne and Jamie! Just sign up to my mailing list, and I'll send *Honor on the Cape* to your email for download to your favorite reading device!

BTW . . . all of my series are inter-connected.

Hugs, loves, & peanut butter!
MK

To all the hopeless romantics...

CHAPTER 1

Sage Mathews held the lacy, barely-there panties to her waist, angling one way and then the next to best show off the simple lines. "Are these really edible? I mean, wouldn't a guy get indigestion or, at the very least, gas?"

Alora Kingsley, Sage's cousin, coughed in her hand, then pretended to pick at a piece of lint that was most certainly not on her bold, floral, off-the-shoulder boho blouse. "I'm sure I have no idea what you're talking about."

Sage rolled her eyes, then looked around Blayne MacCaffrey Astor's store. Eclectic Finds Boutique—Cape Van Buren's premier one-stop shop for everything fun had expanded to include items that inspired a good time on the horizontal, backwards, upside down, or hanging from the rafters, depending on the level of adventure—was newly remodeled and gleaming with all things sexy. And Alora had put her hands on all of it.

"Oh, please. You two have sex-tested every lingerie style in this shop, and I know, for a fact, Maxine Van Buren cheered you on all the way. Hell, she barely let you finish before asking you to write a glowing review for Blayne's store. I know, because she pointed them out to me in the Squeal section of the *The Van Buren Tribune* over breakfast this morning," Sage accused. "I almost choked to death on my coffee, thanks to you."

Alora snatched the panties in a huff but couldn't hide the blush creeping up her cheeks. "It's not my fault. My new bend-friend has been hell-bent on checking out each new style ever since Blayne added the roller derby inspired selection. Besides, the reviews were anonymous."

"There's nothing any more anonymous about Adora than there was about Brangelina. Even if you were secretly dating Adam," Sage said with a pointed glare, teasing about the nickname Cape Van Buren had given to Alora and Adam when they were spotted together in the North Cove Park in a rather tight embrace. It wouldn't normally have been noticed except Adam MacKenzie was CVB 9's weatherman bringing wet dreams to any woman in town with a pulse.

"And I don't think that's what Grandpa Horace had in mind when Yelp inspired him to add the Squeal section to the *Tribune*." Though, in all honesty, Sage could see how the reviews were paying off with every new customer walking into Blayne Astor's store. Blayne had considered closing Eclectic Finds when she thought she was moving back to Glengarriff, Ireland, but Alora's genius management and marketing skills and fresh ideas gave Blayne the security to not only keep it open but expand—that and her new life married to James Astor and living six months in the US and six in Glengarriff.

Sage could only imagine such a life.

But ever since, business had never been better. And, of course, it hadn't hurt that Alora

had landed the hottest bachelor this side of the Atlantic. Happily ever afters all around.

Which was exactly why Sage had moved to town a few months ago. It was her turn. In her new hometown, with its history of successful love matches on the books, she couldn't fail. When you need money, you go to a bank; when you need love, you go to Cape Van Buren.

She looked wistfully at the beautiful bra and panty sets with a critical artist's eye. If she wanted to inspire love beyond the greeting cards she designed, she should start by showing off her best visible assets.

Alora swiped a finger over her cell. "Aren't you going to be late?"

Sage jerked away from the seductive trance of underpants and grabbed the phone. "Crap. Yes!"

They bolted onto the sidewalks of Cape Van Buren arm in arm, like they did when they were six. Sage peeked at her friend and smiled. Every time she had come to town to stay with her grandpa, she and Alora had been attached at the hip. Some things never changed—and she was thankful.

"I'm so proud of you for getting the cartoonist position at the paper. Your grandfather would be glowing with that ear-to-ear grin of his." Alora shook her head with an amused look on her face. "I've never seen another grin as big."

Sage nodded, picturing his deeply lined, weathered face with his shock of silver whiskers and kind, brown eyes as he'd greet her with his usual, "Morning, Hershey Kiss." All the feels washed over her, and it took a second to answer. She swallowed past the lump in her throat. "He would, wouldn't he? It relieves a lot of stress. I can actually handle my rent now, working for both the paper and the greeting card company."

Growing up, she had been sent off on the weekends to hang out with Grandpa Horace, and she had loved every minute of it. While he'd set the printing press for the Sunday paper, she'd explored each floor, had drawn in the art studio, and headed important meetings in the boardroom. And every one of her imaginary friends had been quite satisfied with the management—if she did say so herself.

But even more significant, Grandpa had introduced her to the Sunday comics. And he had been the first to give her a hard kick in the seat, telling her to go after her dreams when her parents had wanted her to do something more practical. Now, she was the cartoonist at *The Van Buren Tribune*, an associate product designer of Share the Love greeting cards, and she would save her grandfather's legacy, if it was the last thing she did—with the help of the new consultant the board was bringing in, of course.

Her grandfather had put a board together—headed by his best friend, Banon Edwards—to oversee the running of the paper after he'd first fallen ill. And now, a stroll across Van Buren Blvd brought them to the *The Van Buren Tribune* and the meeting that would introduce Sage to her knight in shining armor. Ever since her grandfather had passed a little over a year ago, the paper's revenue had been in a steady decline, kind of like the breasts of Cape Van Buren's geriatric sector until introduced to the magic of wearing a sexy bra by Maxine—if she could snag a judge at the age of grandmother, then there was hope for them all.

The board had decided to bring in an expert to try to save the newspaper, and Sage's job. She just hoped he was up to the task. The thrill of possibilities beat a steady *da,dum, da, dum* in her chest.

She grinned as they walked, breathing in the salty, ocean breeze. "I just know today is going to be one for the books. There's love in the air, Alora, and not just from the activities in *your* underpants."

Alora's eyes widened in a pained expression. "Sage. Oh, my God. I swear, if—"

Sage shot up her hand to stop her. "Whoa."

Alora's gaze followed the direction of Sage's, then fell on the same delightful distraction that had made the rude interruption so necessary. "Holy shit." A sleek, black Chevy Impala—the kind they drooled over on *Supernatural*, not the modern-day mundane model spotted in every elementary school's kiss-and-ride line—cruised by, then took a left just past the fire station.

Sage placed a hand to her heart. "I mean..."

"That's an understatement," Alora agreed.

Driving the sexy-ass car was a sexier-ass man. Wind-swept light brown hair framed the classic straight nose and square jaw found on every superhero known to women's dreams. Full lips crooked up at one corner as bright blue eyes lit on Sage, whisking over her from head to toe with obvious interest.

Suddenly, Sage needed a fan—in March.

"Did those eyes just say, 'take me to bed,' or am I imagining things?" she whispered.

"You're not crazy." Alora agreed, echoing the tone.

"Do you think that's him?"

Alora nudged her to get moving. "If it is, your job just got a whole heck of a lot hotter." She pulled back. "Why are we whispering?"

A small wave of goosebumps washed over Sage's skin as her Masters of Fine Arts degree colored her perspective. "Because you always whisper in the presence of a Da Vinci."

Her cousin performed a mock gag and grabbed her by the arm. "Ohmygod, come on. You can't meet your new boyfriend-in-shining-armor unless we get your ass over to the paper."

~

*P*arker Edwards did a quick study of the leggy brunette on the street corner and whistled with pure biological appreciation. If that was what he could expect while taking care of this job in Tiny Town, Maine, then this trip was definitely pointed in the same direction as his...

He shook his head and adjusted in the worn-in-just-right leather seat of his baby. That was exactly the kind of thinking that would get his ass sent back to New York and his grandfather to disown him, once and for all.

Time to man-up and earn the reputation he had for being the best. And even that was still in question by Banon James Edwards I. Being named as one of the Top 100 Internet Innovators didn't mean a thing to the pretentious old bastard. Of course, the man couldn't sing the praises of his name sake loud enough. His older brother was solidly positioned in the family business like the finishing block of the ultimate Tetris game. As the heir, he was a master at towing the accepted family line. But Parker felt sorry for him. He never saw a smile on his brother's face.

Parking his car as far away from other cars as he could in the too-narrow parking lot of *The Van Buren Tribune,* he scanned the clean lines of the print press building. It stood as tall as the Cape Van Buren Fire Station but only a third of the length. Half of the roof rose on a slight, rounded incline and the other shot up on a flat line at a forty-five-degree angle. The walls were floor-to-ceiling glass, giving outsiders an unobstructed view in—and there it was, the tell-tale sign of a small town. Everyone's business was dinner conversation and secrets were as common as hookers on the corner of Garden Parkway SW and Town Square Drive by the police station.

They didn't exist.

He couldn't see Cape Van Buren's badged bad-asses allowing one hint of impropriety in front of their department building—and wasn't that a damn shame?

Sighing, he slid his large frame from his car. Well, for the next week, he was stuck in Tiny Town with the task of saving the newspaper from closing down. Should be a fairly straight forward gig, but an important one. The owner had been one of his grandfather's best friends. They'd grown up together, but Banon had moved away, only to come back after Horace had died.

The old man would never have placed the job in Parker's hands, but the board said otherwise. Now, his grandfather would finally have to admit his grandson's success.

As Parker made his way inside, he thought he caught another glimpse of those mile-long legs through the glass and shook his head. When he glanced back, there were no legs in sight. Must have been a dream, but like his grandfather always said, *Get your head out of your ass, boy.*

The man was so supportive.

Parker pulled open the heavy glass double doors of the paper and blinked twice.

Apparently, his imagination was keener than he'd given it credit for. The long legs in question were planted squarely, supporting the biggest welcome sign he'd ever seen. And a set of the kindest eyes he'd ever had the privilege of witnessing peeked at him from around one side like a kid asking Santa for a new pony.

The sign was an incredible rendition of the *The Van Buren Tribune* building with the sun's reflection off the many glass windows. But the safety net drawn underneath in a webbing that spelled "Edwards" almost made him miss the step up and fall flat on his face. He righted himself with a cool brush of his shirt front and cleared his throat as an uncomfortable prickly sensation settled along his spine. He recognized it and didn't like it one bit.

Expectation.

Gritting his teeth, he forced out a smile that probably looked as strained as it felt. The leggy brunette moved the sign to the side and, with a jab of her thumb and a grin, said, "See what I did there?"

God help him. She thought the web with his name spelled in it was clever.

Another woman with a crazy halo of brown curls, and a decidedly better read on the situation, stood close by with narrowed eyes. "This doesn't look good, Sage."

Staring straight at him with a dreamy smile on her face, the woman called Sage whispered, "The hell it doesn't." Then, she snapped her mouth shut and dropped the sign.

Ignoring her own whispered statement—which Parker found all too interesting despite the warning bells clanging in his head—she stepped forward with a dreamy-eyed look on her face and thrust out her hand.

"Welcome to the *The Van Buren Tribune*. I'm Sage Mathews, the cartoonist and granddaughter to the late Horace Rosewater. I have such great ideas for you." She jerked her chin in the direction of her companion. "And Alora, here, is a marketing genius. I know we can get this thing turned around."

With a looming dread, he took her hand, surprised when she squeezed firmly. There was nothing that drove him crazier than a limp-dick handshake. But with the feel of her silky palm against his—as loudly as his brain told him to steer clear of this too-eager brunette beauty with the elevated expectations, and the never-knew-a-stranger smile—his body told him that one thing was already for certain, nothing about this woman had ever caused anything to go limp.

Which could be a problem.

The other woman stepped up, extending her hand and breaking the weird over-the-rainbow spell he'd been under. "I'm Adora...er, I mean, Alora...Kingsley." She was so tiny, he had a hard time figuring out how she supported such a mop of curls without toppling over.

He raised a brow. "You don't know?"

Funny, her handshake was pleasant enough but not distracting in the least. Feeling a bit more himself, he released her, enjoying the furrow in her brow.

"Not enough coffee..." She waved her hands in dismissal. "Anyway. Not important. I'm Sage's cousin. Well, second cousin." She looked at Sage. "How does it work?"

Sage stared at her for a second, then shook her head with a WTF look in her eyes. "I don't know, however many cousins it works out to when my grandfather is your grandmother's husband's sister's late husband...second? Third?"

He watched them in wonder over familial genetics. Until hearing the two talk, he'd never pair the long legs to heaven with the petite bohemian firecracker as cousins any day. Listening to the two blather on left no room for confusion, but his head was still spinning.

Rubbing the back of his neck, he swallowed a sigh. He had a sinking feeling Sage Mathews was going to be a much bigger problem than his grandfather any day.

If the saccharine look of hope in his welcome party's eyes was any indication, Tiny Town just got a helluva lot more complicated.

CHAPTER 2

S age paced the length of her art studio with one pencil behind her ear, a second securing her hair on the top of her head, and a third held at the ends by both hands. One of the perks of working for the paper was her super awesome corner office art studio that happened to have a fantastic view of the fire station.

Snap!

Alora jumped. "Okay, calm down." She slid from the stool in front of Sage's expansive drawing desk and moved to the window. "Tell me exactly what they said."

Sage tossed the offending pencil into the trash can, pretending it was an arrogant, unoriginal, and now disappointingly sexy, Parker Edwards. "His way to save the paper is to go digital. And I have to show him around Cape Van Buren to help him get a feel for the community and the kind of events we cover. She slid onto her stool, allowing the smooth seat to calm her sizzling nerves.

She was most herself with a pencil in her hand and the scent of graphite in the air. Pulling a long sheet of drawing paper in front of her, she secured it to her desk.

"I hate to say it, but he might not be wrong," Alora said.

Sage threw her pencil at her.

"Hey!" Alora batted it away. "You could poke my damn eye out."

"Oh well, it's not like you read the paper anyway." Sage blinked rapidly, determined not to let her disappointment get the best of her. "How can you say that? You knew Grandpa Horace, and how much he loved bringing the news of our community into the homes as if we're one big, happy family. Digitizing it will only turn it into one of the millions of generic news streetwalkers let loose on the interwebs, and we'll simply be its pimp." Her shoulders fell. "Not to mention, the comics aren't the comics without the warm smell of newspaper ink and the relaxing texture of the newsprint between your fingers."

She stared out the window lost in memories. Grandpa Horace would pat his leg every Sunday morning as soon as he saw her wild bed-head walk into the kitchen. At the table would be her orange juice in a crystal tumbler and his coffee in a favorite, *Don't bother me or you'll end up in my newspaper* mug. She'd sat on his lap until she got too big and had to sit on the chair next to him. His laugh echoed in her head, leaving a heavy weight in her chest.

"I don't think it would work out quite like that, Sage. Maxine and the North Cove Mavens, hell the South Cove Madams too, are all on Snapchat and Instagram, and God help us all, a new mature dating sight called Kindling. It's supposed to be all the heat but none of the assholes. They don't got time for that." She repeated the tag-line with a shudder.

The North Cove Mavens were a group of ladies who lived north of the Cape and sparred good-naturedly over superiority with the South Cove Madams. Something about two sisters who had lived on opposite sides of the town and the one boy who had captured both their hearts. The feud's history was as old as the town itself. Sage didn't know them well enough to trust they'd save anything.

"It would work out exactly like that, and you know it. As it is, half the people in this town stroll the sidewalks barely missing the lampposts because their noses are nostril-deep in their cell phones. This world's going to hell in a handbasket."

Alora rolled her eyes and walked over to the desk. Cocking her head to the side, she turned the comic Sage was working on to face her. "First of all, you sound like you need to join Maxine and the North Cove Mavens talking like that. And second..." She dropped her voice to the one that had accused Sage numerous times of stealing her favorite pair of earrings whenever they spent the night together at Grandie Evette's, "What the hell is this?"

Pulling her shoulders back, Sage gave a stiff shake of her head. "Surely, I have no idea what you're talking about. This is simply a new comic concept I'm working on."

"It has a gorilla stomping through the *Tribune* building with the name tag 'Edward' on his chest. That's not very subtle."

Sage opened her mouth to defend herself but snapped it shut. The next few days had been planned out so perfectly, that was until she found out her too-sexy knight-in-shining-armor was unforgivably tarnished. During the board meeting, she'd tried to offer ideas on a proposed growth agenda, insight on advertising that she'd gleaned from Alora, and even offered her own janitorial volunteer services to help offset some of the cost until the *Tribune* was on solid ground again.

But all the damn silver-tops just stared at her as if they wondered who invited her to the meeting, and Mr. New York had joined them with his damn square jaw and take-your-dress-off eyes. She wasn't stupid, the paper needed to make some changes, but if they thought digitizing the very thing that glued the community together was the answer, they were all seriously blinded by their own self-important bullshit.

Finishing out the drawing to her satisfaction, she examined it from a few different angles, then held it up for Alora to look at. "Good. I wouldn't want the big, dumb animal to get confused."

Alora put her arm around Sage's shoulders. It was both supportive and judgmental at the same time. "You know...they say you catch more flies with honey than vinegar."

"I don't want to catch any damn flies."

"But what about finding your long-time-coming love match in Cape Van Buren?"

Sage lifted one corner of her lip in a scowl. "Well, it certainly won't be with Mr. Parker Edwards. I can't abide ignorance." She flicked her hand at the rows of glass windows that made up her office wall. "I'll just have to keep my eyes peeled for the right fire-boy."

Alora sucked in a breath. "Dayummmmmm."

Both ladies straightened, then leaned over the desk as far as they could. There, on the patch of groomed lawn between the station and the paper, was a firetruck getting a sponge bath.

By six of Cape Van Vuren's finest.

They were overgrown with mounds of muscle that certainly would need a good evening rubbing and fine-chiseled features that made Sage's lips curl into a smile with all the dream potential. She grinned. "I just need to get me one of those."

Alora's nod was slow and slack-jawed. "Now, I know why you don't want the paper to digitize...with this view, 'hot off the presses' has a whole new meaning."

⌇

*P*arker clenched his jaw to keep from saying what he really wanted to his grandfather, deciding to begin with the one word that couldn't cause him any trouble. "Grandfather."

"Mr. Edwards, for God's sake. We're at work, not the county fair."

Parker wouldn't be surprised if his teeth crushed under the tension radiating from his jaw. No one else was even in the damn conference room, or at the paper, for that matter. The day's edition had been printed the evening before and sat ready to go. The decline of the *The Van Buren Tribune* had nothing to do with the work ethic of its employees.

It was six o'clock on Friday morning.

And business hours weren't until eight.

But to his grandfather, business never stopped, never paused, and never ended. For anything.

Period.

So, he was there to work, which meant Parker had to be as well.

"Mr. Edwards." He enunciated his name slowly. "I understand the board feels it's necessary that I research the town with Miss Mathews, but I'm confident that I can handle it on my own."

His grandfather tossed the paper he was looking over onto the long, oval table, then folded his hands in front of him. "Well, apparently *they* aren't."

"I didn't see it that way at all. I feel they think they're helping, but she'll just get in the way."

His grandfather pushed up from the table. "You do understand that you aren't here because of me, but because of the board's misguided loyalty to myself and Horace. I would have gone in another direction. Used someone completely clear of the family."

The shame that always accompanied Parker's conversations with his grandfather crawled up his back, vertebra by vertebra. "I'm sure you would have. Putting family first has never been your priority."

Consistent with his grandfather's true form, he gathered all of his self-righteous rage behind his blue eyes, but kept his face serene. "You will follow the board's wishes, and that's final. One problem. One misstep. That's all I need to suggest we find another consultant." The only clues he was upset were the slight shake in his deep voice, the intensity pushing from his gaze, and years of being on the receiving end of the man's verbal lashings.

Parker snapped the back of his patent leather Italian dress shoes together and saluted the old man. "Sir, yes, sir." Sometimes, he wondered why he even tried. He was so much like his father, there was no way his grandfather would ever really see him as anything but a constant reminder of the old man's failings. And if Banon James Edwards I felt like he was failing, he made everyone around him pay.

Not waiting to be dismissed, Parker grabbed one of the papers from a stack on the table and headed down to the large front lobby to take advantage of the early-morning silence. It didn't have the privacy of an office, but it was about as far from the conference room as he could get. He worked on refining his strategy of data-gathering to ensure the recommendations he made at the end of next week were not only spot-on but inspired—both satisfying to the people of Tiny Town and the board members' budget constraints.

The sun continued to climb and, finally, he pushed back from his laptop to stretch, resting his arms along the back of the sofa. The Friday edition of the *Tribune* rested next to him on the pewter, herringbone-patterned cushion. He eyed the paper as if it were the cause of all his problems.

Let's see what Tiny Town has to offer.

Spreading the paper on the coffee table before him, he devoured each page.

The usual nuptials and deaths were listed, but so were birthdays. There was no crime to speak of, unless you counted a boat-napping that was actually just a prank from some guy named Ryker Van Buren against Mitch Brennan over something that had to do with a moose.

What the hell?

Parker chuckled as he read through the story. He and his brother were friendly. They spoke on holidays, birthdays, and any time they had to sign documents pertaining to the Edwards empires, but they weren't friends. The idea of it all was a bit over-the-top, making him yearn for the sequin-dipped sidewalks, dirty skyscrapers, and compromised dreams of New York.

But then, Sage's hopeful smile popped into his head, and he had to shake her out.

This whole town seemed to be drunk on romance and fat on love.

He flipped the paper over to the back, finding the day's comic along the top edge.

"Sonofabitch!"

Shoving his laptop into his bag, he grabbed the damn paper like it was a cobra ready to strike. Dropping the bag strap over his shoulder, he marched out of his new glass house.

Thanks to the local events section, he knew exactly where to find the little brat.

Down the sidewalk and around the corner was as far as he had to go. The Cape Van Buren Fire Station was having a pancake breakfast to raise funds, and one Sage Mathews was running the griddle.

With the front doors wide open, he could already hear the laughter and merriment brought on by too much sugar downed with too much caffeine. He worked his way through the crowd until he found the legs he was looking for visible behind a tall buffet table set with three portable griddles. Sage ran through the lines of pancakes like she was flipping cards at a poker table.

"Can I help you?" His field of view was suddenly blocked by a man the size of a damn lobster boat, with the name tag "Mayor Marth". But where Parker's size was grown fiber by fiber at the gym, this guy's appeared to be a freak of nature, if the sheer breadth of his shoulders in the well-tailored suit were any indication.

"No, man. I'm just here to have a word with Miss Mathews."

The guy grabbed his shoulder and steered him toward the opposite side of the large, open room. "The names Sebastian, I'm the Mayor. I hear you just got to town and met with Sage and Alora, something about saving the *Tribune*."

The feisty bright-colored sprite could be seen loading pancakes onto pink and red paper plates next to Sage. He nodded. "I have."

"Look, I only want to help, and I'm telling you...the last thing you want to do is go talk to Sage..." He waved toward Parker's face. "With that I-wanna-kill-

13

someone-or-something look on your ugly mug when she has her girls all around her."

Parker studied the guy for a beat, noting both his humor and sincerity, then dipped his chin. "I appreciate it, but I also feel like if I give that woman an inch, she'll take a mile." Then, with a handshake and a thank you, he set off toward the sweet smell of pancake batter and the telltale scent of newspaper ink.

"You're right, and she'll hang you with it." The Mayor laughed but didn't try to warn him off again.

Parker understood. They were a small town, all the wives were friends, they all had Sunday dinners together and kid's birthday parties, but he wasn't from here. So, the last thing he worried about was a bunch of pretty women.

That thought completed itself as he stepped up to the buffet table, and he faced the cousins. Another woman—who looked more like Sage's cousin with her long, dark hair than Harper did—joined them. How the hell did one little town have so many hotties in such a small square mile?

These fine specimens would make the ladies in New York run to check their make-up and change their clothes three more times before being seen in the same room.

"Miss Mathews, we have a problem." He slapped the paper onto the table, noting that it would not be going back with him. Not now, when it was surely caked in batter splatter.

Sage's eyes barely flicked toward the paper, then locked on his, and the friendly energy from yesterday was replaced by a laser-focused chocolate ray of dislike. "We most certainly do, Mr. Edwards. So, why don't you do us a favor? Since you're so good at fixing things, why don't you take care of our problem and get your backstabbing ass out of our fire station?" She finished on a sweet note of sarcastic respect.

He shoved his finger onto the gorilla's chest. "What the hell kind of game are you playing with this comic?"

She rolled her eyes. "It's a comic, Mr. Edwards."

He hated how she said "Mr. Edwards." It sounded too damn much like how he said it when he was speaking to his grandfather.

Wiping her hands on a pink towel that read, *if it's too hot in the kitchen, call Cape Van Buren's Fire Department*, she leaned over the table with a very distracting display of cleavage peaking from the top edge of her apron, her tone all but dripping over the pancakes, "A comic strip's purpose is to tell an amusing story. Big, dumb animals are amusing."

He looked over the drawing's big, goofy-faced gorilla with the name tag "Edward" on his chest, smashing the newspaper building. There was no mistaking the story she was telling. His grandfather would have a stroke. It was all the man needed to have Parker fired.

"You need to knock off the childish tactics. We're supposed to be working together, in fact, you welcomed me with open arms yesterday." Even to his own ears, his tone was rising from accusing to a hint of demanding. He cleared his throat.

The last thing he needed was Banon I on his ass because of Tiny Town's color-by-number comic. "Look..." He stepped forward. "Take your coloring book—"

"No, sweet thing. You look." The other woman who'd joined Sage and Alora stepped in front of him. Had he been paying attention earlier, he'd have noted both the vintage biker jacket and the warning look in her eyes. But he certainly noticed now. "This is a family affair, and you're not invited. Sage isn't stuck holding your hand around town until tomorrow."

"Family affair? From the looks of it, the whole town is here."

"Exactly." She stepped close, almost nose to nose. "And I'm warning you, one wrong move..." She flicked a butter knife at his crotch, and he died a little inside. "And you'll be leaving on a higher note than you came in. I roller derby and, at this point, ridding the world of one mere man would be child's play."

His balls shrunk faster than the time a hot blonde—with both an ass and rack competing for number one—talked him into taking a polar ice plunge.

He tried to retreat as far as possible away from the weapon. Butter knife or not, balls and blades were never meant to meet.

"Blayne, stop." Alora laughed, not even trying to hide her amusement for the sake of politeness.

Sage just watched with an all-too-satisfied smirk on her face.

Parker skimmed his eyes over Sage from the top of the hair piled high on her head, to the fire in her eyes, and on down to the Ugg slipper boots on her feet, liking what he saw a helluva lot more than he should—his dick never did have a lick of sense—and pointed to the paper.

"You're only making my decision easier."

15

CHAPTER 3

*T*he next morning, Sage gave a sharp nod of determination, then walked toward Parker with a smile pasted on her face, a plan in her heart, and a strategy in her head. She'd spent the night gleefully replaying his look of horror when Blayne had threatened his precious with a butter knife.

Maybe she should feel bad but should didn't always lead to did. Especially when he was messing with her newspaper and calling her comic a coloring book. Her teeth ground tight, and she wiggled her jaw a bit to force it to relax.

If only he could see the importance of Grandpa Horace's vision. It was more than just the news. It was a way of life, a part of the happily ever after she was determined to find, and Parker was trying to destroy it all before it had a chance to begin.

But she'd open his eyes.

And what incredible eyes they were.

As she approached Mr. New York, her legs threatened to give out. Cape Van Buren boasted a lifestyle of *work to play* in a community that was really good at slipping on a pair of Bean boots to clean a boat or fix a fence, so she didn't see many suits around her circles. Though, she had when she'd lived in the city and never thought much about it.

But now, the desire to give a low, slow whistle that was all meat-market and no class made her lips tremble. Pressing them together, she resisted—barely. One thing was for certain, she hadn't known what she was missing when a suit was filled out. Parker Edwards in dress slacks that formed to his muscular thighs like a hug, and a pressed shirt that showed off his muscles more than concealed them, made her seriously consider if she'd ever seen a real man before.

Well, no doubt, he fit the bill. She'd always been told that men were animals, and Parker happened to be the big, dumb gorilla type. At least, that's what she liked to tell herself to ease the not-so-subtle quiver in her stomach.

Because holy hell in one of Janice Brennan's floral handbaskets, the man gave Cape Van Buren's finest a run for their money—and this town was full of hot men.

She cleared her throat. "Truce?"

His jaw flexed a few times as he assessed her from head to toe, making her skinny jeans feel a little too skinny, and her dark brown sweater less roomy than she'd remembered.

"I wasn't the one at war."

She fell in step next to him as they made their way toward the large, open green space in Van Buren Square. "You want to destroy my grandfather's legacy." Her words were quiet but firm.

He grabbed her arm and turned her toward him, sending a little thrill straight to her middle.

"I don't. I want to save it. Turning small newspapers around is my specialty, and I'm damn good at it. I don't understand why this is such a big deal. The point is to keep the paper alive. You can draw anywhere. It's not like it's your livelihood. My job is."

Not her livelihood? He didn't understand a damn thing, which was embarrassing. But the passion in his voice was unexpected, almost as much as the cowlick at the part of his hair that was stubbornly sticking in the opposite direction from the rest.

Her fingers itched to fix it and, at the same time, she tried to figure out who he was trying to convince. The assertive tone in his voice spoke of something much larger than her opinion.

Shoving her hands behind her back to both remove the heat left from his hand and keep her from touching his hair like the weirdo she was trying so hard not to be wanted to do, she argued, "But, *The Van Buren Tribune* creates family, it unites us."

"And that won't change."

Iridescent dream bubbles floated about her head and popped one at a time. Because yes, it would change. All of it.

"Now, more than ever, the paper needs experience and business savvy to keep it relevant."

"Business savvy? And what you don't think that's possible in small town Cape Van Buren?"

He gave an indulgent nod. "Your words not mine."

And she wanted to knock him on his smug ass.

"So you think you're what? More savvy? Sophisticated, maybe? Unable to be manipulated or duped or whatever you *businessmen* do to win?" She said the word like it was a contagious infection.

"Haven't yet."

She pulled in a deep breath of ocean air, loving the scent filling her nostrils and relieved it had the same calming effect as every time before.

Her position as the cartoonist for the paper, making a home in Cape Van Buren, and her grand idea of ever finding a man to look at her like Jay Astor looked at Blayne seemed more like a cruel joke than a possibility at this point.

Words piled against her closed lips like rocks in an avalanche, but she swallowed them down. An idea took shape, pushing a giggle up her throat. Arguing would do nothing but make them late for the Vino Pairing Picnic that Dine on the Vine was throwing to launch their newest wine. They were blowing past wanting to be a premier winery into being one of the most sought-after cellars in the world, but Marco Bonamici always put the town first. The wine started and ended with Cape Van Buren. Just like family.

Words had their place. But when it came to this community, Parker would have to *feel* it.

Pulling in a breath, she let go of every argument she'd prepared for the day and pulled him toward the soon-to-be party.

The feel of his large hand in hers was startling. Her palm was curiously sensitive to the calluses that ran along his, and her fingers twitched with the need to rub against his skin.

Pull yourself together, woman.

She released him before she embarrassed herself.

The large, open lawn was polka-dotted with round tables and heat lamps rented from the fire station. The navy cloth napkins stood out against the white tablecloths and were placed around centerpieces of grape bunches twined with ivy leaves. Marco was setting up a cheese tray at one of the many tasting booths that ran the perimeter of the park and Dine on the Vine employees were unloading boxes of wine.

Sage rubbed her hands. This was one of her favorite events, and the universe had blessed them with the perfect day, the sun shining high in the sky with the welcoming cry of the seagulls heard from overhead.

Moby, the baby moose that had imprinted on Evette Kingsley, was dressed in rose-bedazzled collar and tied next to a Cape Van Buren Fire Department metal trough. True to form, it looked as though the animal was working steadily on the knot of the rope. He kept finding his way back to town no matter how far out Cape Van Buren Wild Life Rescue had tried to relocate him. Until they could figure out what to do, they tried their best to manage him. Thank goodness he wasn't yet fully grown.

Blayne spotted them walking up and pulled Jay along beside her. "Isn't this great?" Ignoring Parker, she looked pointedly at Sage and pulled her in for a hug.

Finally, she spared Mr. New York. a glance, then she flicked her hand at belt level, the reflection of the late morning sun glinting off a cheese knife this time. "Just so you don't forget."

Jay groaned and grabbed it out of his wife's hand, giving Parker a silent man-to-man apology. "Leave the poor guy alone. He's just doing his job."

"You're lucky you grabbed the blade, or you'd be next," Blayne threatened Jay with her hands on her hips.

He yanked her up against his body. "The only thing you're going to be cutting me with is that sharp-ass mouth of yours." And before she could answer, he swooped in for a kiss.

Sage swore if someone opened her chest at that moment, hundreds of little hearts would float out in a love-drunk waltz. It might be crazy, most would definitely say corny, but she just couldn't help it. This is what she was looking for.

Someday, anyway. She pulled in a breath, then forced a smile on Parker. "See? Family."

The look on his face screamed *get me the hell out of here*, but he didn't resist as she grabbed his hand. This time, he even gripped hers a bit tighter, making goosebumps shoot up her arm any time his fingers moved against her skin. She was hopeless. "Let's go check out the tasting booths and see what else is going on. They're just about set up, and as soon as noon rolls around, this park will be shoulder to shoulder, Cape Van Buren style."

"God help me," he mumbled.

Sage heard him but chose to ignore it. Not everyone appreciated how amazing small-town living could be. Heck, she'd resisted it herself for a long time. But carving out her own space in the city was like trying to find room in a sardine can.

And the dating. She shuddered. Out of sheer desperation, she'd tried one of those speed dating lunches. The first guy asked her bra size, the second guy asked if she was into open relationships, and the third guy wanted to know if she had any brothers. She was about as successful at dating as Evette was at keeping her moose on a leash.

"Look out!"

Sage grabbed Parker, and a look of pure horror crossed his face as if the devil himself barreled down on them with hooves, a large furry snout, and massive shoulders. "What the hell is that?"

"A nightmare."

Parker threw his arms around her, then pivoted until they both went flying. Somehow, he tucked her against him and rolled them out of the path of insanity.

"Moby!"

She could hear the commotion of trying to wrangle the beast, but all she could see were the buttons on Parker's shirt, and all she could feel was the delicious weight of him sprawled out on top of her, making it hard to focus.

The proverbial dust—which, in this case, was dormant blades of grass and a few rose petals that must have fallen from Mittens' picnic collar—settled around them like a snow fall at the end of a romantic movie.

"What just happened?" Parker asked, gasping. His eyes were wide, dilated, and the brightest blue Sage had ever seen. His chest rose and fell with large volumes of air, which crushed her breasts in the most intriguing way. He'd yet to realize he was still on top of her. She would tell him to move. Really, she would.

As soon as she could breathe again. Because the feel of his massive chest, the scent of his cologne, and the fact his mouth was mere inches from hers, had stolen her breath and made her lips tingle as if zapped with an electrical current —whether she wanted it to or not.

"Are you okay?" he asked, shoving his fingers through her hair and skimming her skull.

Shivers of delight raced across her scalp and down her neck.

Who the heck ever thought her head could be so sensitive? She grabbed at his hands to still them before she asked him to keep going. "Stop. I'm fine. I'm fine. Besides, I was the one who was supposed to save you."

He stilled, looking closely at her face. "Save me?"

"Of course."

"You're not kidding," he said in a tone of disbelief.

"Why would I be kidding?"

Those baby blues dropped to her mouth and stayed there so long, she almost raised her head to close the distance, but then, they lowered to the cleavage pushed up from the weight of him on her chest. Her cheeks flushed, and she tried to make light of their position.

"Well, this is one way to change your mind that I hadn't thought of." As soon as the words were out of her mouth, she wanted to swallow them whole. What the hell? Did she really just joke about propositioning him—with sex?

That was not how she operated. Besides, the last woman he'd ever want would be to have sex with was some cartoonist who was making his job harder. Making his pants harder, on the other hand…

Wait. What? The feel of his body against her thigh burned, and she couldn't help shifting against him.

His eyes snapped back to her face, dilating further and proving she wasn't mistaken. Something warm and heady bubbled up in her chest.

Lifting himself from her, he stood, brushing at the front of his shirt and his dress slacks. Large, brown patches of earth and grass stains colored each elbow and his right shoulder from the fall.

Desperate to change the subject, she joined him and swiped at his shirt with short, jerky movements. "I can get this out for you. I'm so sorry." She continued to swipe blades of grass from the front of his chest, intrigued by the hard muscle she felt beneath. At this point, she was sure her blush had passed her hairline and was fast on its way down her back and to her ass by now.

This time, he grabbed her hands. "It's okay."

She shoved them behind her back, then searched for Moby. Jerking her chin in the direction from which they'd come, she said, "There he is, damn trouble-maker."

Parker raised a brow. "Moby?"

"Like I said…boys are dumb animals."

He nudged her, then laced her arm through his. "Show me more, but regardless of how fun it was to wrestle you to the ground, can we stay on our feet this time?"

The square filled as more and more of Cape Van Buren's residents came for a swallow of vino and a savory mouthful of cheese. This was a crowd that treated samples like a smorgasbord, and Marco was prepared.

Lines began to form at each tasting booth; each one represented a certain grape and with it, the perfect pairings of sweet, savory, and delicious—thanks to the concerted efforts of Delizios and the North Cove Confectionery.

Sage narrated as they went, introducing Parker to shop owners, and showing him how many of the businesses pulled together to give the people of Cape Van Buren something special.

"And this is a regular thing?" he asked.

She shook her head, swiping a small wedge of blue cheese from a sample plate along with a small wine glass filled with a heavy, aromatic dark red. "Is what regular?"

Parker waved his hand around the event. "This. The crowds of people, the businesses working to help one another. Is it like this for every event, or is there something different about this one, in particular?"

Sage took a bite of the cheese, letting it melt against her tongue. "Ohmygosh. You have to try this."

She held it to his lips.

With something akin to confusion in his eyes, he glanced from her to the cheese, then opened his mouth. She popped the cheese in, then pulled her hand away, but not before his lips had closed around the tip of a finger. A sharp tingle shot through her hand as the feel of his generous, warm lips imprinted on her memory.

He closed his eyes while he rolled the small bite around in his mouth. "This is amazing."

Yes, it was. She blinked. Oh, the cheese, of course.

Sipping from the wine glass, she hoped it would yank her over-active libido back down to Earth. She handed him the glass, praying he wouldn't notice it trembling. "Try this with it. Marco's a genius when it comes to pairing his wines with just the right food."

He tipped the wine back, emptying the glass, but then, let it settle in his mouth before he swallowed. "You're not lying." Glancing from booth to booth, then out toward all the tables now filled with towns folk, his lips quirked up. "Huh. For such a small town, this wine packs a pretty big punch."

She tried to keep her irritation out of her voice. "You're so focused on the fact we're a small town. We may be small, but we're progressive, with growing businesses, and a passion for caring for every person in this town. All you have to do is walk down the street to see it. Or visit the Archer Conservation Park of Cape Van Buren. But besides that," she waved her hand, "Dine on the Vine and the wine they produce are in demand all over the world now."

Pride swelled her chest. Their success had nothing to do with her, but living in Cape Van Buren meant everyone celebrated everyone else.

And they also gave her hope.

Hope that she'd find her own one day. She thought of the comic samples she'd sent to Andrews McMeel Publishing. The idea of publishing in the same house as *The Far Side* was as likely as getting Moby to ever go home or behave, but she'd gone for it anyway. And every day she waited to hear back was agony. Parker might think her comic was nothing more than an over-rated coloring book, but it was so much more. Comics were both her passion and her dream.

He didn't even bother masking the surprise in his voice. "Really?"

Sage turned toward his condescending tone, the now common sensation of frustration tightening in her chest further. At the rate her emotions were tracking around this guy, she was going to end up at the Van Buren Memorial with a panic attack before the week was up.

If he didn't see this town as significant, he wouldn't care less about its small, local paper.

"What did you think you'd find, coming here? Bonanza?" She narrowed her gaze. "This town is filled with hardworking professionals who aren't afraid to get dirty or meet a challenge head-on."

Shoving his hands in his pockets, he smirked. "I'm sure the local professionals *are* challenged."

With level-headed poise her grandfather would be proud of, she set her plan in motion. "Cute. But this town isn't afraid of anything. Our North Cove Plunge proves it."

He raised a brow. "Are we done here?"

Shit. He wasn't taking the bate. Disappointment raced through her like Moby had the park.

"So, this North Cove Plunge. What is it exactly?"

And just like that, her day turned around.

CHAPTER 4

$\mathcal{W}$hat did he think he'd find?

Parker set the wine glass down on a nearby bussing table, then grabbed another and downed it in one swallow.

Even thrown back, that was one helluva good wine.

He studied the iridescence in Sage's eyes. It was as though they were made of glass and the dark chocolate of her iris reflected light instead of absorbing it. He clenched his jaw in the hopes of crushing his wayward thoughts with the effort. Holy Christ. The last thing he needed was to let any of the romantic bullshit of his new sexy and distracting friend get inside his head.

He sure as shit never imagined he'd find a hopeless romantic in Tiny Town who could make his dick stand tall and sing the national anthem, but one feel of her soft, giving body under his and it was like he was sixteen again and Sally Rogers let him get to second base. It had been over before it even started, and the little debacle a moment ago wasn't really any better.

Who was he kidding? It had been great.

Sage's curves had snuggled into him as if *he* were home, and God help him, if it hadn't taken every ounce of effort he possessed to keep from kissing her or feeling just how silky her skin was above the lace of her fancy bra peeking out from the V-neck of her sweater.

For a moment, he'd been sure *she* might even kiss him.

But when she brought attention to it all with her attempt at humorous innuendo, his body shot to attention like a damn cannon, knocking a little sense into him.

Tangling the sheets with the granddaughter of his grandfather's best friend was the last thing he should do. Even thinking about it sounded complicated. He was here for a job. One that he was more than qualified to do. And he'd kick ass and do it without giving his grandfather any more reason to throw his judgments around. In the end, the old man would have to acknowledge Parker's success, even if he was too proud to admit it.

But Parker would know.

Once and for all.

And then, he'd let the man go.

If he didn't want Parker in his life, the reason for staying in the old man's became less and less clear.

"Sage Mathews, we need your help." There was no mistaking the wisdom in the voice, nor the do-as-I-say tone.

Sage stiffened next to him. "Oh God, I don't like the sound of this at all."

"I don't understand," he said.

"I don't either yet, but I'm afraid we will." Sage waved at two older women pinning them down with determined looks in their eyes. "Hey there, Grandie Evette, Miss Maxine."

Parker did a double take as he took in the two women dressed in matching bright black bustiers over striped black and wine colored, fitted skirts. He'd never seen so much cleavage from someone called Grandie before —or Maxine, for that matter—though, he had to admit, it gave him hope for his seventies.

"Grandie?" he asked.

Sage smiled. "She's my great auntie by way of marriage…Grandie."

"But wouldn't that be more like Grantie?"

She rolled her eyes. "I nicknamed her when I was four, okay?" The strain in her voice almost made him chuckle. Something was up.

"We need your help." The two ladies stopped side by side.

"Parker, this is my great auntie, Evette Kingsley. She's the owner of the North Cove Confectionery on the corner opposite the Flat Iron Coffeehouse, and this is her best friend, Maxine Van Buren…you can guess her significance."

Then, gesturing toward Parker, she continued, "Grandie, this is Parker Edwards. He's Banon Edwards' grandson."

Evette sucked in a breath, and for a moment, he was afraid she was going to pass out from asphyxiation. "Banon Edwards? That old coot?"

Parker winced.

Sage stared at Evette as if she didn't recognize her for a moment. "And the gentleman responsible for saving the *Tribune*."

It was interesting that, though Sage said the words, it was loud and clear she didn't believe it. What would it take to convince her that he had the paper's best interest in mind? In the end, it really didn't matter. The job would get done and get done right, then, he'd be hightailing it back to New York where everyone did not, in fact, know his name—just as he preferred it.

And where brown-eyed girls with hearts floating above their heads didn't give him a hard-on. He needed to get back to the land of sanity—STAT.

The mission of the day was to tread carefully and placate Sage as much as possible just to ensure no more gorillas named Edward popped up in the paper. Then, he could get back to doing the job he was hired to do.

"Edwards, why does that name sound so familiar?" Evette patted her smoot, looking like a pin-up Olive Oyl.

"Grandie, I just told you."

Evette skimmed the front of her bustier. "No, no. That's not it. By the way, how do you like my advertising for Blayne? We thought of asking you and Alora to do it, but Lord knows how the two of you get all atwitter when we mention sex. So, of course, Maxine was a no-brainer."

Maxine waved her jeweled fingers with a suggestive grin.

Parker coughed in his hand. Maybe it hadn't been an innuendo when he and Sage were on the ground after all.

But Sage's look of mortification cleared up any confusion. "Grandie!"

Evette poked her finger in the air. "Your comic. That's it. I think you got a winner with that one. That gorilla, Edward, is hysterical."

Parker rolled his eyes as Sage raised her brows with an agreeing nod. "It really is," she answered, grabbing on tight to the change in subject if the forced smile on her face was any indication.

"Anyway, we're wasting time. Which us North Cove Mavens don't like to do." She tsked. "We need you for the kissing booth."

Sage glanced over one shoulder, then the other, until a look of pure horror crossed her face. "Me?" she squealed quietly, pointing at her own chest. Shaking her head, she brushed past her great aunt. "Oh, heck no. I am not doing that."

"Just for a short bit." Evette hooked her arm through Sage's and led her on down the path with Parker and Maxine hot on their heels. "Maxine will throw in some of her moonshine."

Moonshine? This was going to be good, and there was no way in hell he was missing a second of it.

As it was, the two looked ridiculous with the struggle it took to keep Sage in line with Ms. Kingsley's heaving bosom almost popping out of her top. So much cleavage for such a thin woman.

"Jade Dawson's on her break, the other two triplets are out of town, and Larkin and Claire are off-limits. Blayne might agree just to drive Jay crazy, but she had to run over to her store and meet with Alora. You're the only other single lady I got right this second."

"No way. Grandie, I am not sitting in Eclectic Finds Kataclysmic Kissing booth."

"I told you she'd be a negative Nelly," Maxine said. "Who'd of guessed the younger generations would be the prudes of our town?"

"Hey!" Sage threw her hands up.

They arrived at the booth and Parker whistled. It was decked out in some of Eclectic Finds newest romantic additions, and the thought that Sage should model the goods instead of doling out kisses popped in his head before he could stop it.

Evette placed a hand to Sage's cheek. "But the proceeds go to the Cape's Coping through Art program. You know how much this would mean to Claire. Besides, where would you be if Horace hadn't introduced you to your love of art?"

Sage's eyes widened like a sad cartoon character's where the light reflected and wobbled in the corners. The sight hurt his feelings, and he almost stepped in to volunteer. But just in time, clarity returned, and he found his balls again.

Fuck, he'd lose his man-card before escaping this town if he wasn't careful.

"Fine." She stomped behind the booth. "But you owe me."

No sooner had Sage stepped behind the counter, and it seemed just about every guy in town bee-lined their way to the booth as if their dicks had honey radars. The hell he'd let any of these clowns get one taste of that full mouth.

And he'd deal with why in another century.

He slid up to the booth and slapped a hundred-dollar bill to the counter. "This should cover you."

"Well, isn't this interesting," Evette yelled, not even trying to be subtle. "Hey, Maxine. See what we got here? I wish Janice was here to see this."

Parker ignored the watching women. For some reason, seeing Sage kiss a line-up of different men made his gut twist. Did it make sense? Hell no, but what did in this damn town?

Sage leaned toward him. "What are you doing?" she asked in a fierce whisper. "Don't you think my humiliation is bad enough as it is?"

He'd let her hurtful words pass; she was reacting under stress and hadn't been privy to a kiss from Parker Edwards before. Well, he was about to make her day. Actually, he just wanted to save her from having to lock lips with every Tom, Dick, and whoever the Harry-hell else was lined up behind him. "I'm trying to help you, you spoiled brat. Don't you think a hundred dollars should cover your friend's break?"

Sage glanced down at the money under his hand. "A hundred dollars, are you crazy?"

He'd never thought so, but since stepping foot into Tiny Town, he now had serious doubts.

"Well, get on with it already. There's a line," Evette demanded.

Sage's eyes grew wide, and her mouth parted in a small "o."

He winked at her. "Let's make it a good one. Give your paper something to talk about."

A mischievous twinkle lit her eyes, and her mouth widened in a grin.

Dropping a hundred-dollar bill might look like a sacrifice, but he bet those lips tasted like a reward.

Snaking his hand beneath her hair, he gripped her neck and dropped his mouth gently to hers. He'd been wrong, her lips tasted more like a celebration, one that had the potential to never end. She was sweet with wine and possessed a slick heat that made his body snap to attention.

He'd had every intention of pulling away, but her arms snuck up around his neck, and she dove in like she'd just discovered scuba diving—and he was going with her. She angled her head, sliding her mouth against his, and as she broke away just enough to sample from another angle, he grasped the opportunity to take a deeper taste.

When his tongue touched hers, her body jerked and her arms tensed, all but pulling him over the counter, and he wanted nothing more than for the crowd to disappear so they could see where this was going in private.

Because he sure as hell liked the direction

"What the hell is going on here? Is this a festival or a damned orgy?" Banon James Edwards I stood in a wide stance, his arms crossed at his chest, and condemnation on his face. Pretty much his usual look.

Parker drew back from Sage, then stepped between her and his grandfather like a protective wall. She didn't need any of his shit directed at her. "Sir, you know that's uncalled for."

"What I'd say is uncalled for is embarrassing our family's name."

Evette Kingsley sashayed around the booth with her head held almost as high as her bosom, then stepped between him and his grandfather, with Maxine at her side, like two love sentries. "Now, you listen here, old man. Your grandson just donated one hundred dollars to our youth art program. What exactly have you done?" She poked a bony finger to his chest.

Parker had never seen his grandfather uncertain, but at that moment, the old man looked like he wanted to run, and he couldn't make eye contact to save his life.

"Her eyes are up there, Edwards." Maxine poked her pointer and middle fingers toward her friend's face.

"Excuse, me. I was—"

"Yes, you were what…here to tell your grandson 'nice work?' Here to make a donation? Or here to ask me out on a date?" Evette questioned casually as if she had similar conversations every day.

Parker all but choked on his own tongue as his grandfather's mouth opened and closed like a fish out of water. No one had ever spoken to the old man like that, none that ever survived anyway. Parker never thought he'd see the day, but there his grandfather was, given what for by a woman dressed in her street corner best and all the poor guy could do was stare.

Banon Edwards cleared his throat. "If you'll excuse me."

Evette laughed and shook her head. "I'll be waiting. You know where to reach me. I'll save you a cupcake."

She turned toward Parker and Sage with a self-satisfied grin and the devil in her eyes. "He wants me."

"Grandie!" Sage pressed a hand to her mouth, looking from Parker to her aunt as if she were trying to figure out who to run from first.

Maxine nodded in pure appreciation. "Now, that's how a Maven hunts its prey."

A tiny blonde with a friendly grin and even friendlier eyes joined them. "I'm back." She hugged Sage while she inspected him from head to toe. "Thanks for the help, Sage. Looks I've got my work cut out for me." A look of *challenge accepted* crossed her face as she examined the long line of suitors.

She crooked her finger toward Parker. "You can be first."

Sage stepped up and grabbed his hand. "You got your hands full already, Jade."

He glanced down at Sage, surprised by the strong tug in the other direction. Waving at the ladies, he let her lead him away. "In a hurry?"

"To get you away from a Dawson Triplet?" She scoffed. "Yes."

The idea that she didn't want him kissing the woman named Jade made him feel a shit-ton better about his donation. Though, if they were both feeling it, the reality was, he had more of a problem than he thought.

They made their way through the crowds of tasters with Sage not letting up on her grip of his hand. And he didn't mind—which was weird as hell. He'd never been a hand-holder, even with women he'd been dating a couple of weeks, much less a couple of days.

Shit.

He and Sage weren't even dating.

Watching her out of the corner of his eye, he noted the perfect tip of her nose, and how she was the perfect height for him to see just a bit down her shirt, and how her smile left his chest tight. The afternoon was not at all what he'd expected, starting with how caring of a person Sage was right down to how good she tasted. The fact that his grandfather just got hit on by a corseted septuagenarian couldn't even register. He shook his head.

"I'm sorry," Sage whispered.

"For what?"

"This isn't exactly how today was supposed to go. And your grandfather seemed really mad."

That was an understatement. Monday would be a long day of ass-chewing either by his grandfather or the board. He had some fast-talking to do to make sure they didn't replace him. He rubbed the back of his neck. "Yeah, well. He's not my greatest fan. But I owe Evette a big one. I've never seen the man run scared in my life. It was fucking awesome." The last statement was punctuated with a fist pump, and Sage jumped.

"Oh!" She continued with a fearful look in her eye, "Don't tell Grandie you owe her, the reality of her payout might give you nightmares. She'll consult with Maxine." Laughing, she shook her head. "Family is as terrifying as they are beautiful."

But that was just it. He didn't know beautiful, not when it came to family. Though each day spent in this town was giving him a glimpse of what being a part of a larger whole could really mean.

It was another reason to finish this job and hightail it far away. No sense in sampling something he could never have.

But despite his best efforts, he couldn't look away from the gratitude and joy shining from those damn chocolate eyes.

CHAPTER 5

*J*ust as the sun was rising, the next day, Sage stood on the north side of the cape and clapped her hands together in feigned excitement. "Are you ready?"

She tried to keep her voice casual against the bubbling sensation of glee rising up her throat. She hadn't thought he'd take the bait, but he hadn't been able to help it. And that's what she'd counted on.

But she hadn't counted on how affected she'd be after that damned kiss.

And now, faced with the one responsible for her night of tossing and turning with dreams she wouldn't even share with Alora, she almost wanted to fess up to the prank she was about to pull off.

Almost.

"Look, if you all can do it, I can do it," he said.

She held back her eyeroll. Parker needed a reminder that her town was relevant, powerful, and not insignificant just because it wasn't a metropolitan. In fact, it was more so. The intimacy of a town like this allowed them to work more closely in business. Which left them with some of the most successful commerce on the east coast.

It was time to loosen him up a bit, show him not to underestimate her because she was a small-town newspaper cartoonist.

He jogged in place trying to keep warm as the waves of the Atlantic rushed upon the shore in a bubbling froth. Six a.m. in March was not the warmest time to go for a swim.

Sage couldn't wait to see his face. That is if he actually went through with the challenge.

"I'm as ready as I'll ever be. So, I'm supposed to dive into the freezing ocean. That's it? Not quite a challenge if you ask me."

The better-than-thou tone of his voice washed away the tiny nibbling teeth of guilt, making her lie easy. "The story goes that if you can withstand the freezing waves of the Atlantic, you can withstand anything. Sailors and lobstermen originating from the Cape have done it for centuries to give them good luck before setting sail."

She unzipped her fleece and kicked off her athletic pants. His eyes roved slowly up her body, and her nipples peeked against the material of her swimsuit in resentment of the cold rather than the heat of his gaze. She was sure of it.

Normally there'd be no way she'd be caught dead in a bikini in freezing temperatures, but she was determined to sell this North Cove plunge and put Mr. Edwards in his place.

He blew hot air in his hands and rubbed them together. "That's quite the story."

"Our town is full of them." She pointed to the farthest peek off the cliff across the waters. "See that overlook at the very tip of the land over there? The one that begins the North Cove? It's known as Truth Point. Anyone looking for the truth, with a pure heart, can figuratively attach the question to a rock and ask for the truth to be revealed as the rock is thrown into the sea."

His loud laugh caused an answering call from a few seagulls.

She stepped up next to him trying not to give him the same once-over as he pulled the thick sweatshirt over his head. But her eyes refused to listen to reason and devoured every inch of smooth skin. As he shoved the running pants over his hips, she swallowed hard. And every memory of that kiss slammed into her.

Suddenly the cold Atlantic breeze wasn't cold enough, and she felt like she needed the ice-cold plunge herself.

Shaking the silliness from her head, she shook her hands. "This is it!"

She was counting on his strong sense of competition for her little prank to be successful.

"Okay, on the count of three."

"I'm ready," he said. "But for the record, you Mainers are crazy."

She laughed with a nod. "Wicked crazy. Don't you ever forget it. One!" she shouted.

"Two!" And pulled her arms into running position.

"Three!" She shoved off her back foot in a sprint toward the water. Her burst of speed got him moving, and as suspected, he shot ahead of her.

She pulled up short and watched, enjoying the view of his back muscles contracting with each pump of his arms, and his calves bunching into mounds the size of softballs as he pushed off the gravelly sand.

He was a fine specimen.

Running through the water, he shouted in shock but still dove through the waves.

She grabbed her sweatshirt, reveling in the look of surprise on his face as he surfaced to find her still on dry land.

"What the hell?" He put his hands up and immediately trudged toward the shore.

She was laughing so hard she doubled over at the waist. "The look on your face!"

Success!

"Are you kidding me? You could have given me hypothermia."

Tears of hilarity ran down her face as she said, "You look fine to me."

"What the hell was this all about?" He stormed towards her over the sand.

"I don't know Mr. High-and-Mighty-City-Slicker, but it looks to me like you just got played by a simple, small town…girl."

Suddenly, she was yanked against his chest, her sweatshirt falling to the rocky ground.

On a squeal, she grabbed onto his shoulders. "Hey!"

"If I'm cold and wet, you're cold and wet, you little brat." But instead of being pissed, he sounded amused, and her heart turned over. Resisting her struggles to get free, he even laughed. Not many men she'd come across over the years would ever have taken such a prank so casually.

Her grandfather had always told her to look out for a man with a sense of humor. "Humor is a sign of a good man, Hershey Kiss." With the soft echoing memory of her grandfather's voice in her head, she blinked twice, then focused on Parker's face.

The feel of his hard chest against hers and his scent clouding her head, left her feeling a bit high and thinking impossible things.

Like how much she didn't want him to let her go.

Instead of leaving her cold, his ocean-cooled skin and the Atlantic winds were a much needed relief from the fire raging in her body. Her little prank hadn't taught him a lesson at all. But it sure as shit taught her one.

He didn't leave her cold at all, only wet.

~

Two days later, Sage had to bite her lip to keep from whistling as the wanting to be held in Parker's arms again grew at a steady, relentless pace. She still couldn't believe how well he'd taken her little joke. Or that she'd been successful.

"I was afraid you were avoiding me."

He snorted. "Where are we going anyway? I don't trust you for a minute." Parker walked up in a pair of worn jeans that hugged his thighs, and Sage would bet her cartoonist salary—measly as it was—that they celebrated his ass, too.

"Aww, come on. You know you deserved it. Your cocky level has been sky high since you got here."

He stopped short. "*My* cocky level?"

"Okay, okay. Point taken. But I have a good reason," she said, pushing down any residual guilt from her prank.

"So do I."

Dipping her chin in acknowledgment, she slid her arm through his, relieved when he didn't pull away. She was treating him to one of Claire Adam's, soon to be Claire Brennan's, art lessons at the new center out on the Cape. Claire's program, in addition to her event planning business, had become so popular across all ages, she hadn't been able to teach general classes as often as she'd like, so this was a special treat. And one more way for Parker to see how the paper was significant to the Cape Van Buren's way of life.

"I'm glad you wore some casual clothes. But we're going to have to do something about that button-up."

He glanced down at his light blue designer shirt, brushing his hands over the front. "What's wrong with my shirt?"

"Not a thing as long as you keep rubbing it that way." Her eyes popped wide. Damn it! "I mean, aren't you afraid of getting paint on it? I'm not sure Armani goes with candy apple red acrylics."

He visibly blanched.

Laughing, she grabbed his hand. "Don't worry, we'll think of something." At least, she hoped she would, anything besides how good he tasted and better he felt. She couldn't get the damn mind-numbing experience of kissing him or being held in his arms out of her head, and they were going on over forty-eight hours since her lady parts had started singing hallelujah. It was distracting.

He'd taken Sunday for research—or so he'd said. Sage had worried the whole time he was avoiding her because of the kiss or the joke. Or both. She was sure the last thing he wanted was to get sexy with a *small-town* cartoonist, but damn if she didn't wish it anyway.

Then Yesterday, he'd been holed-up with the board in meetings in the morning and then in the evening. She'd seen him for all of two hours mid-day at the Cape lighthouse alongside a gaggle of kids who'd been visiting on a field trip. Thank God the kids had been there because every time she stood too close to him, her lady parts leaned his way like a damn divining rod. The only thing keeping her from making a complete fool of herself was the threat of jail for indecency in front of minors.

In the end, the extra hours alone left her a lot of time to work and too much time to think. She'd planned a new series of greeting cards and had made progress on the week's comics. Unfortunately, her apartment studio's walls were also now beginning to look like some weird stalker's altar of worship with the different profiles of Parker she'd drawn. But there was something in his eyes that she couldn't quite place just by looking at him—so she'd needed to draw him. Pencil to paper in multiple shades was where she got her answers.

Thanks to the success of Saturday's picnic, there were so many hearts floating about her head that even her comic gorilla, Edward, was behaving himself—somewhat, anyway. The Sunday edition showed the big oaf kissing the townsfolk while being chased down by Moby the Moose, and Monday's edition was Edward playing hide-and-seek with the children in the lighthouse.

That one really got to her. When she'd taken him out there to show off everything Larkin and Ryker had accomplished, she never imagined he would actually interact and play with the children, and even look like he enjoyed it. Her heart had gone a pitter-pattering, rudely refusing to listen to reason, common sense, or any words, period.

She sighed and directed him up the front steps of the Victorian and into newly renovated Cape house, noting that his jeans did, in fact, celebrate his ass and gave a small fist pump of victory.

Holy shit on an apple stick, how did a man in business get a body like that? She fanned her face, dropping her hand quickly as he turned toward her.

"Are you feeling okay?" he asked, dipping his head to find her eyes.

Which now stared at his fully packed crotch instead of his round and ready ass. It took all the X chromosomes she possessed to drag her eyes up to meet his. "Oh, of course. I was just, um..."

"Great, you're both here." Claire hopped up from her desk in the large front room washed in neutral tones and hints of the sea to meet them, and Sage made a mental note to thank her later. "The kids are so excited to meet Edward. I mean, Mr. Edwards."

But Parker hadn't missed the joke and shook his head with a lopsided grin. "If you guys are honestly teaching these kids that I'm the gorilla, you two are bad influences."

Sage giggled behind her hand. "Oh, I almost forgot. He can't get paint on his shirt, and with these kids, that's like saying don't breathe. Any ideas?"

Claire looked him up and down with a gleam in her eye. "Follow me."

They marched through the foyer to the bathroom at the backside of the house. "Take your shirt off."

"What?" Both Sage and Parker said, simultaneously. Though Parker also leaned forward with a look of pure confusion on his face.

"Your shirt. You don't want it stained, take it off."

He blinked at Claire.

"Oh, for sweet carrots and brussels sprouts, I'm not going to photograph you for the Eclectic Finds next underwear ad, I'm going to give you a smock."

"Sweet carrots and brussels sprouts?" Sage asked.

Claire rolled her eyes. "Don't you start with me, I have to keep up the habit so I don't slip around the kiddos.'"

Parker joined it. "I gotta side with Sage on this one."

Sage's heart warmed. "Even after what I did?"

"What did you do?" Claire asked.

With a shake of his head that said, *these women are crazy* more than it said *I should stay quiet*, Parker released the buttons of his shirt, revealing solid mounds of tanned, smooth muscle from underneath.

And with each button let loose, Sage lost another breath.

"Sage."

Damn, she thought he was sexy before, but this was beyond anything she'd ever imagined.

"Sage," Claire said a little louder, holding out a smock. "Help him out instead of eye-banging him."

"Ohmygod! What happened to sweet carrots and brussels sprouts? There are kids out there."

"Exactly, and the more time I spend in here, the more likely they are to tear the place down."

Sticking her tongue out, Sage grabbed the smock. It was one of the many hospital gowns donated from Van Buren Memorial. Wanting to die of abject mortification, Sage twirled a finger at Parker, handing him the cover-up. "Put this on, I'll tie it in the back."

He remained generously quiet as he shrugged into the foam green material. Every striation in his back stood out with each movement, and Sage had to swallow—hard. "That's ah...I mean. You must work out."

What? Why did she keep opening her mouth? She needed one of Grandie's to shove in it to keep her quiet.

Grabbing the ties, she threw them into a knot, then turned to flee, but Parker stopped her with a hand to her wrist. "It's the gym. I work out to release stress. And you have the worst poker face I've ever witnessed in a human being before. I gotta say, it's kinda adorable." The soft rumble of his voice skittered up her spine.

Great. She held back a sigh. She was adorable. Like a damned puppy.

"Shut up." She scowled, but only halfway before a grin joined it. "Come on."

All the kids hailed the new arrivals with the excitement and acceptance that only the single-digiters knew how to do.

Claire introduced the class to Parker and Sage, then got everyone moving along. The sharp, clean smell of acrylic hit Sage's nostrils, immediately making her feel at home. When she sat down to work, she most often used a black, felt-

39

tip Flair pen on twenty-four pound Southworth bond paper, but acrylics on poster board worked for her, too.

She peeked at Parker to find him making faces at a little girl with a face full of freckles and two missing front teeth. Her cheeks were rosy with delight as she stuck her tongue out, pulling her lips wide with her fingers at the same time.

"Miss Maggie, are you going to play or paint?" Claire asked, then turned toward Parker. "I'm hoping you won't be a distraction, Mr. Edwards?"

The whole class giggled as Parker replied, "Yes, Miss Claire." Then, he threw a wink toward Maggie and picked up his brush.

Sage applied bright yellow paint to her brush, then added her first stroke to the blank page. The first mark was always the most exciting one and carved the path for the rest to follow.

She'd seen so much more of Parker in such a short period of time, and it was becoming more and more difficult to envision him as her adversary. Especially with those bedroom eyes, and that sexy as heck grin. He was hardworking, kind and open. He played with the children and flirted with the likes of Evette and Maxine. And even though Jade and every other eligible card-carrying estrogen oozer followed him around like he was the newest lobster on a stick at The Lobster House—not that Sage cared, of course—he'd politely offered a hello, then had moved along.

Sage couldn't remember a time when she'd ever seen Jade stare forlornly; that was a woman who got what she wanted when she wanted it. But Sage saw it Saturday.

"Where do you draw?" he asked, pulling her from her daydreams and back to the much less interesting present—as far as reality went, anyway. He found her adorable. Great.

"I have a studio in my apartment."

"So, did you share the hobby with your grandfather?"

Gripping her paint brush to keep from throwing it at him, she bit her lip. Art wasn't her hobby; it was who she was. How could he miss that?

"Can I see it?" he whispered, oblivious to how close he'd come to being throttled.

She stared at him, distracted from revenge by his question, as Claire continued to give instructions and "ooh'd" and "aah'd" at every student's masterpiece.

Sage never let anyone but Alora in her work space, and a tight sensation wrapped around her chest. It was too personal, too intimate, too special—with more than her work. It held all the best memories of her childhood with her grandfather. Not to mention the new art on her wall. But something in her wanted to show Parker. He really seemed to be understanding the importance of the paper to Cape Van Buren. And to her. Even if he didn't understand the importance of her art.

Maybe, if she let him in, he'd really see the light. As soon as she removed the drawings of him, of course.

And she wasn't too blinded by her own agenda to miss the struggle Parker had with his grandfather. She didn't understand exactly what was going on, but the old man sure didn't seem to hold his grandson in very high regard, which only made Sage think the poor thing was going senile.

Claire clapped her hands. "Thank you so much for this special treat. It's nice to see you all improving since the last time I taught. Remember, it's not the art you make, but the *you* made by your art."

As the children cleaned their work stations, Claire hurried up to Sage. "Hey, can you lock up, Blayne called and needs me to pop over to the store real quick."

Sage nodded. "Of course."

Clearing the space and organizing the paintings with eight children was like herding cats through a catnip field, but eventually, Sage shut the front door and took in the beautiful Atlantic view out the front window. "Phew," she said with a hand to her brow.

"It's been a busy week," Parker said, leaning against the archway leading into the kitchen.

She nodded, suddenly aware of the intense look in his eyes, the fact that he'd dropped the smock, and the decadent sensation of being alone with him sending goosebumps along her skin. "Hopefully, you see how important this place is."

She stopped before him, threw her arms out to the sides, then let them drop. Her fingers itched to trail along the fine hairs running from his navel down to his belt buckle.

"What do you say about showing me your studio?" He tucked a stray hair behind her ear.

"I'd say I'm scared."

His eyes held hers while his thumb traced her lower lip.

41

She shivered but didn't back away. "It's like stripping naked."

His hand dropped to her shoulder, then snaked around the back of her neck. "I really want to see you naked."

He did?

Drawing her to him, he walked them toward the back hallway and pressed his mouth to hers.

His skin was smooth and seared her fingertips in the most delicious way. She wanted her hands everywhere and all at once.

He was hot, sweet, and demanding. His tongue stroked against her own, and his hands roamed over her back and down her hips until they grabbed her bottom through the smooth fabric of her silk skirt, forcing a small whimper of *"oh my God"* to escape her mouth.

With his hands massaging her ass like that, her panties would never be the same again.

Her body tightened with need, and as his fingers slid up her side and covered her breast with a delicate squeeze, she groaned into his mouth. This was everything and so much more. Apparently, being adorable was a good thing.

That was all it took to unleash something she'd not witnessed before. With all his delicious weight, he pressed her up against the wall, lifting her legs until they circled his waist. His heat was hard and persistent, and she yanked him closer still, in hopes of relieving the rising tide of pressure at her center.

"I want..." she whispered against his mouth, loving the scent of him...the taste...how he felt under hands and against her skin.

"Tell me," he demanded.

"I want you to..."

"What you want is to get your asses out of the *public* Cape center, you sickos, and come help Blayne with a shipment."

Like a cold trough of water dumped over them, Alora's voice all but drowned Sage.

Parker stilled, then dropped his forehead to hers as she slid her legs back to the ground.

Clearing his throat, he opened his mouth to speak.

"Save it. I think I've seen enough and would rather not hear the narration," Alora said, though the grin she directed Sage's way was definitely more fist pump than punch in the face.

Parker locked eyes with Sage, telling her he wasn't anywhere near being finished.

But Alora waved to them over her shoulder. "Come on. Claire sent me to get you. And you owe me. I just saved you from having to face the new Cape house caretaker. Or did you forget there are people here twenty-four hours a day?" She directed the question to Sage but then turned to Parker. "I'm cashing in. It's time you see what it means to live in Cape Van Buren."

Sage couldn't read the now neutral expression on Parker's face. What was she going to do with him? He was trying to make his grandfather proud, and she was trying to save her grandfather's legacy.

She had a bad feeling one of them had to lose, but God help her if that didn't give her the strength to keep her hands to herself.

CHAPTER 6

Sage had never walked through Eclectic Finds horny before. It made every piece from silk and lace to breast salt and pepper shakers and one of a kind blown wine decanters more decadent than she'd ever imagined. Suddenly, she could feel the cool, slippery fabric sliding across her skin and the hot press of too tight leather holding her just in the right place—all without trying on one single garment.

"Come on slow pokes, what the hell were you three doing over there, having an orgy?"

Sage choked. "Maxine!" Though it wasn't a bad idea—just her and Parker, of course, and not in a public place. Nothing inspired the hot and heavy like Blayne's new collection. She fanned her face. Maybe she'd give him a personal tour as soon as they were finished helping Maxine with whatever she had going on this time.

Maxine put her hands on her hips, making her well-tailored jacket open in the front, revealing another bustier. She may have added a new staple to her wardrobe. The woman always dressed to impress.

And it was one of the things Sage admired about the woman who knew this town so well.

She was her own woman, living to please herself. She did what she wanted, said what she wanted, and really lived life in the way that spoke to her. And she never let anyone put limitations on how she did it.

Sage had never told her, but she thought it was one of the most romantic things she'd ever witnessed. Maxine had a love affair with herself that every woman should have. And she kept the relationship strong even now that she'd married Judge Theodore Carter.

Not that was a wedding to remember. Sage had captured wonderful photos that she hoped to work into a comic for her new project.

Their story was known from the north cove to the south and was not spoken of outside their happy nuptials if those involved ever wanted another sip of her amazing moonshine.

"How can we help you, Ms. Van Buren?" Parker asked.

Maxine brightened. "Now, that is what I like to hear. Come on, boy." She guided the trio down the hall to the storage room, filling Sage with a whole slew of ideas, as she stared at Parker's backside in front of her.

"Where's Blayne and Claire?" Sage asked Alora.

"Blayne is with Larkin working on some project, and Claire had to meet Mitch."

Claire and Mitch. Sage held back her sigh. It was nice to see the two of them together. Claire'd had a hard road when her fiancé had been killed in the same car accident a few years ago that had taken Larkin's first husband. Soon after, Claire had also lost her unborn child. Too much sorrow for one heart.

But she'd found another great love in an unlikely heart with Mitch Brennan, the town's once upon a time most eligible bachelor turned dedicated city attorney.

That's what Sage loved about this town. The impossible was reality in Cape Van Buren.

"By the by, Evette's got her eye on your grandpa. Any chance you can put in a good word for her?" Maxine asked with a hopeful expression as if it were the most normal conversation to have with a young man she hardly knew.

Parker's eyes almost crossed. "My grandfather? Banon Edwards?" He scratched the side of his head. "I thought that whole scene at the wine pairing was a joke."

"My dear boy, you have a lot to learn about the women of Cape Van Buren,"

Maxine said, as she led them to a row of stacked boxes. "Evette Kingsley is single and ready to mingle. It's about time the North Cove Mavens get back out there."

She pulled out a box cutter and slit the throat of the first cardboard victim. "And what she wants is to mingle with your grandpa's dingle."

"Ohmygosh, Maxine! I swear you get more shocking every day. On purpose," Alora laughed.

"You cannot say those kinds of things to Mr. Edwards. He's trying to save Grandpa Horace's paper." The heat in Sage's face had gone from mortified to kill me now, and Claire didn't help one bit, all but busting her gut from laughing so hard.

"Better you than me," Alora said with a shake of her head.

Parker wasn't sure where to look and visibly appeared as if he might throw up.

She grabbed a trash can. "Here, need this? I often do when I talk to Maxine."

The laugh he gave her was weak with a cry for help echoing within it.

"Help me with this, boy," Maxine demanded. "They'll be some moonshine in it for you later."

Parker jumped to it. Sage assumed from abject fear since he didn't know that Maxine's moonshine was worth just about any mortification known to man.

It was that good.

Alora elbowed Sage in the side and whispered, "That was quite a show."

"Shut up. I bet you and Adam have christened every inch of this place by now."

"Maybe, but you two are so hot for each other boogers, fart jokes, and the threat of being caught didn't even cool you off."

Sage rolled her eyes, choosing to ignore her cousin.

In a more serious tone, Alora asked, "How are things going? Besides the tonsil inspection, I mean." She grinned.

Sage glanced over to see Parker heaving boxes under Maxine's instructions. If she didn't know better, it almost looked as though the woman was having him move the boxes more than he had too. "Is she…"

"Oh yeah, she's watching, making him put on a show. I don't know what is in the water in this place, but the North Cove Mavens have stepped up their I'll-do-what-I-want since Maxine's wedding." Alora said.

Sage resisted groaning out of sheer desperation. "If he doesn't get scared away first, I think he's really starting to see our town, Alora. He's been playing with the children and making friends with the older generation. He sees how we all pull together to make one family instead of a town of families. Ya know?"

"You don't have to convince me. I came home before you, remember?"

"I know." Sage nodded. "I remember when you told me you were moving back. I thought you were crazy even though I'd yet to have one genuine friendship, much less a sincere relationship, in the city." She looked around the back room of Eclectic Finds. "This is home."

She put her hand up. "I mean, this isn't home. It's—"

"Poor Parker's personal Hell?"

Sage followed the direction of Alora's gaze. Maxine had Parker backed into a corner and was feeling his biceps.

"Crap."

As Sage moved to save him, Alora grabbed a box of crotchless panties to unload and inventory. "Adam's going to love this."

"So, tell me your plans for *The Van Buren Tribune*," Maxine asked, as she removed tall gold dipped shot glasses of every color from a box.

"He's still figuring things out, collecting data," Sage said.

Parker took the opportunity to slide out from between Maxine and the wall. Moving a few more boxes aside with his leg, he used the box cutter and opened the rest, one after another.

"Now, this boy knows how to work. Okay, kids. Rack and stack, then we'll get everything out on the floor."

"Happy to help," Parker said. "And to answer your question, Ms. Van Buren—"

"Maxine. It'll make all my friends jealous if they think you see me as a woman."

He winked. "There's no mistaking that...Maxine."

She smiled at Sage. "I like this one."

"Anyway..." Sage laughed.

"With everything I've seen this week..." He glanced at the array of goods surrounding them, then grinned. "And it's been a lot. I think the answer, now more than ever, is to take the *Tribune* online. Most of the folks I've been talking to are already regular users of Facebook and Snapchat—which was a huge surprise for me, to be honest. It wouldn't be anything to create an app that's specific for Cape Van Buren."

"What?"

"Love it!"

Sage and Maxine spoke together.

A death grip tightened around Sage's chest, making it difficult to breathe. All her effort to make sure Parker really saw the true Cape Van Buren suddenly seemed for naught. She showed him it was personal interactions and real intimacies that made her town's heart beat, not a smart phone or laptop.

And he still wanted to cheapen it with gigabytes and URLs?

"Sage, you're crushing the velvet."

She winced. "Sorry." She released her chokehold on the deep purple, place mats. Counting how many had been delivered, she marked the number on the inventory wand that computerized the whole store.

Grabbing another box to empty, she strategized the best way to handle this. If she went off—all boobs, and hair, and fingernails—he'd never listen, but if she hid behind her fear, he wouldn't hear her, either.

She opened another box to find it filled with Come Again condoms.

Inspiration struck.

That was it.

"Parker, let me explain it in terms you'd understand. *The Van Buren Tribune* is like using condoms during sex, where online is more like an unprotected one-night stand."

"Less sensational? I don't really think that's what any paper's going for," he answered, with a *that doesn't sound great at all* look on his face.

A look she really wanted to smack off. Maybe, at this point, she'd just smother him with Grandie's bosom.

She picked up a handful of condoms, then threw them at him.

Lifting his hands, to shield his face, he batted them away, laughing. "You asked."

"I'm with Parker on this one," Maxine added.

Oh, for the love of all that was holy. Sage tried again. "Nooooo," she ground out. "Condoms with sex are a sign of respect, of true caring. They're putting the other person's health and well-being as well as your own in a position of priority and importance. A one-night stand is quick and over and hopefully forgotten.

That's what you'll get if you put the *Sentinel* online. Sex without any connection. Without the making of a family. After the novelty wears off, it'll be forgotten, untouched, and unwanted."

"Damn," Alora breathed. "I've never wanted to read the paper so much in my life."

Sage scowled and threated with another handful of condoms.

Parker broke down the empty boxes as the women finished hanging the lingerie collection on rolling racks. "Sorry, Sage. You're wrong. Taking the paper online is the answer to keeping overhead low and profits high. To keeping your job. I've done this before, and I've run all the numbers. There's no question."

A loud buzzing filled her head. "What do you mean, my job?"

He straightened slowly with a wary expression, and his lips pressed into a thin line. "Didn't they explain that to you? The paper can't afford to stay in print, the only way there's any hope of retaining your job is for the whole system to go online, including your comics—but that isn't guaranteed, either." He put a hand out. "Look, drawing's a hobby, right? Something to do to keep your creative juices flowing. Starving artist and all that? You have other options, don't you? Because there's a chance you'll be drawing for yourself instead of Cape Van Buren."

A hobby? Other options? Where the hell did this arrogant jackass come up with this stuff? He was living in New York, for God's sake, the land of artists and broken dreams.

Broken dreams.

Her heart squeezed so hard at the thought of losing the *Tribune* that it was everything she could do to keep from crying. But she wouldn't. Not in front of Parker. Not in front of the guy who couldn't seem to take what she did for a living seriously.

Then, she thought of her submission to Andrews McMeel Publishing, and all the uncertainty turned her stomach sour and left her head pounding.

"A comic isn't a comic if it's read on a computer screen," she gritted out, her voice tight, and her lids burning. Comic art couldn't be appreciated on a computer screen, she didn't care what the resolution was. Part of the art of a newspaper comic was the newspaper—holding it in her hand, the ink stains on her fingertips, the hot-off-the-press aroma leaving a halo of memories around her head.

Her grandfather's warm smile as he approved her drawings from early on teased in the recesses of her mind. *"You're going to make a fine cartoonist someday, Hershey Kiss."*

She pulled her shoulders back. All thoughts of wanting to give Parker a personal tour after hours vanished, and in their place were thoughts on the best places to bury his body.

Alora laid a comforting hand on her arm.

"Again. I don't agree," Parker said in his all too annoying I-know-better voice.

Well, you're stupid.

That's what she wanted to say, anyway, but until the bottom line was signed and there was nothing left for her to do. She had to preserve the communication between them and hope she could change his mind.

Now, it wasn't just the paper on the line but her job, too.

She had less than five days to train a gorilla.

CHAPTER 7

*P*arker closed his eyes and tried to count backward from ten, but apparently being a big, dumb gorilla made the task impossible. Thursday had come faster than expected, and little miss romantic had curiously demanded very little of him. In fact, she had been quite placating in the past day or two.

He thought it was guilt from the damned *North Cove Plunge*.

She'd gotten him alright. And he'd happily let her get him again if it meant having her in his arms in nothing more than a bikini. Bikinis made some women sexy, but Sage made the bikini. That was for sure.

He studied the newspaper left on his desk.

This time, the sexy little shit drew Edward the gorilla traipsing down Main Street, throwing newspapers on the ground in the new roller derby inspired lingerie set from Eclectic Finds. And it wasn't bad enough that the big, hairy beast wore a bra—with cleavage, but there was a view from behind of the thong, too—with cleavage.

His ass was in *The Van Buren Tribune*, and Banon James Edwards I was not happy.

"Damn it, Parker, I told you not to screw this up."

Rubbing the back of his neck, Parker suppressed a sigh. "I'm not screwing anything up, Mr. Edwards. I can't control what Ms. Mathews illustrates."

His grandfather remained silent.

"Sir."

"The hell you can't. Don't act like an ass, and it won't show up in the paper!" He slammed the paper down on the table. "I've called a meeting with the board. You're an embarrassment to the *Tribune*."

Parker slammed his hand down on the table. "No," he replied in a low tone, doing everything in his power not to yell. "I'm an embarrassment to you. The thing I've never understood is why. I'm not my father. But apparently, you aren't able to separate the two." He straightened, grabbing the paper. "And all this time, I've been running after you as if you were the smart one."

His grandfather's face flushed red. "The board will most certainly—"

Parker gripped the paper tighter, telling himself he could not, in fact, slap some sense into his grandfather, no matter how much the man might need it. But it was hard. His grandfather's constant rejection chipped away at something deep inside, something Parker had been working to rebuild after every visit.

Now, he was more tired than he was hurt from having to defend himself to a man who should know better. "The board will be impressed with the strategy I devised. The board will be thrilled with just how much of a profit margin I've been able to create. I've run the numbers, Mr. Edwards." He couldn't keep the sarcasm out of his message. "And I'm able to give the board more than they asked for. So, tell me...what exactly will the board say?"

"Well, now. You don't really think this conversation is necessary, do you, Banon, honey?" Evette Kingsley marched right through the door of the conference room with a victorious smile on her face and a power play in her lanky step. She no longer had the look of a woman on the hunt, but of one who had her prey right in the palm of her hand. Like Olive Oyl if she owned all the spinach in the world.

If Parker hadn't seen it for himself, no one, not even God himself, would have convinced him to believe it, but his grandfather blushed. With a strained voice, the old man said, "Evette, we talked about this. You can't just show up when I'm working."

"But I needed you, and...I brought you cupcakes." She slid an aromatic box onto the conference table, then yanked at the bottom of her fitted blazer which made her cleavage and Banon's eyes pop. There was no doubt in Parker's mind that Evette had been shopping the new collection at Eclectic Finds, and that his grandfather had just been magically delivered to Lala Land. Damn, cupcakes seemed to work just as well on old men as boobs did on the young ones.

She kissed his grandfather's cheek, taking great pleasure in rubbing the pink lipstick off if the grin on her face was any indication. Sliding her arm through Banon's, she demanded, "Now, leave your grandson alone. He's going to save the *Tribune*, so let him do his job. How could you be anything but proud?"

"Evette, this is a conversation—"

"That you don't want to have because I'm right?" She nodded. "Yeah, I can see that."

She winked at Parker. "Besides, Parker here has a thing for Sage Mathews, and you know how much we all love Sage. Shows the boy's got excellent taste, if you ask me."

A tight grip of panic seized his throat. "I do not have a thing for—"

She raised a brow. "The news I got from Alora yesterday tells me different. It appears the Come Again condoms need to be shared over at the the Cape house as well as Eclectic Finds."

At this point, he wished his grandfather had just fired him, then he wouldn't be suffering through this conversation. The fact was, he didn't do relationships. Certainly not with a woman whose heart floated upon her sleeve, who had the sexiest damn ass he'd ever seen, and whose mouth made men sing Hallelujah. He wanted Sage more than he wanted to make his grandfather proud.

That stopped him cold.

Fuck.

An image of the two of them attending events in the park and helping Claire at the conservation center should have had him heaving in the trash can, but a buzz of warmth vibrated through his chest, instead.

Evette snapped her fingers, and his grandfather snapped to attention. The whole *single and ready to mingle* mantra of one Evette Kingsley had disappeared and been replaced with *she got his dingle in a vice grip* because no one ever told Banon what to do.

Banon escorted her from the conference room. "I'll be just a minute." Closing the door, he turned back to Parker. "Listen to me and listen to me good. Finish the job, then get out of town. I think you've caused enough humiliation to our name, don't you?"

The words weren't new, but the sting was just as strong. Parker studied the old man's face, resisting the urge to rub the raw, burning pain from his own chest. But that was the way of it. He'd never been good enough for the man and never would be.

"Why do you hate me so much?"

His grandfather stared at him with something akin to surprise on his face, but Parker waved his hand in dismissal. "Forget it. I'll be gone by Sunday."

With a nod, his grandfather exited the room with a solid, final *thunk* of the door closing behind him.

Parker stood frozen in his spot for a minute or two, or ten—however long it took to let the tightness in his chest ease and the twisting in his stomach lessen. Checking his watch, he ticked off everything Sage had told him she had to do today, then made a bee-line for her apartment.

He had to see her.

There was something pulling him to her—the kindness in her chocolate eyes, the soft, husky sound when she said his name, the way her face heated when he caught her staring at him. She felt it, too. They might not have forever, but he had to have her now.

He enjoyed his walk through Van Buren square. The sounds of the ocean, seagulls and crashing waves, the briny scent of adventure, ship ropes, and anchors all made for an atmosphere that made promises. Something he couldn't do for Sage.

But damned if he could make his feet turn him around.

Knocking on her apartment door three times, he listened for some sort of movement from inside.

"Coming!"

She pulled the door open, and he was hit with the sweet smell of baked goods and pencils.

"Parker." The smile on her face was like the first step into the shower after a hard day's work.

Without words, she pulled him inside.

He stood back against the door. "I'm sorry I came, I— "

"What is it?"

She stepped toward him, her bare, orange-painted toes, peeking out from beneath a pair of loose-fitting, low-hung jeans. Her California Dreaming t-shirt was a size too small, which was a size just right, stretching across her breasts in a way that made him itch to tear it off.

"I need..."

Pressing her hands against his chest, her touch froze the words in his throat. She slid her hand to the top of his slacks and released his buckle. Is this what he came for? Didn't she deserve more than a one-night stand with a man ready to hightail it back to the city? She did. There was no doubt, but there was also no doubt what he needed.

Her.

She dragged his pants down, then worked on the buttons of his shirt while he dropped his boxer briefs and kicked them to the side. Shoving the shirt from his shoulders, she pressed into him, flattening her breasts against his chest in a way that more than fulfilled every dream he'd had since seeing her holding that damn sign.

It was too much. Snaking his hands into her hair, he pulled her in and slammed his mouth to her parted lips. He slid his tongue against hers—her taste and heat making his brain numb and setting his body on fire. Gripping the hem of her shirt, he leaned back just enough to pull it over her head. "Fuck. I've dreamed of touching you, tasting you."

"I'm here."

He stared into her eyes, and she pushed her jeans to the floor. She wore no panties, and he feared he'd never be able to be around her in jeans again without losing his load. He groaned at the sight of her, then again as her hot palms skimmed across his chest.

"I'm here," she repeated. "With you."

Sliding both hands over the smooth skin of her hips to the two dimples just above her ass, he pulled her in tight. Her soft, slick skin was like every dream he'd ever had but in HD. "God, you feel so good." He slid his tongue along her lower lip, savoring her taste, her texture. She was better than any fine wine or aged Scotch he'd ever sampled.

He dropped to his knees, holding her in place with his hands at her hips.

"Parker," she whispered.

He pressed his lips to the sensitive skin along the apex of her thighs, then trailed his tongue toward her center. Finding home, he settled in. He wanted to memorize every curve, every valley, every inch of her silky skin. With light, feathery flicks of his tongue, he worshipped how she was made. Then, he closed his mouth around her and sucked in a gentle rhythm that left her knees shaking and her chest heaving.

She pulled him up, then pressed him back against the door with plans of her own.

His body was tight and straining, his muscles burning, his mouth watering. He swore she set off a fire in him so hot, Van Buren's firemen didn't stand a chance in hell of putting it out. Anchoring her arms around his shoulders, she wrapped her legs around his waist, and as her body landed flush against his, he broke.

"Look at me," he growled.

She kissed him, pressing and sliding against his body, driving him beyond anything he recognized. "Sage. I mean it...look at me."

Promise shone from her eyes in a way that made him want to dive under and never surface again.

"I see you, Parker. I see you."

CHAPTER 8

*P*arker stared into her eyes, begging her to see who he really was—a man capable of great things, a man with good intentions, a man who sometimes needed to be shown that he was worthy and wanted.

Sage held his gaze until he nodded, then, she lowered her legs and let her body slide slowly back to the ground. "Parker." She held out her hand.

He grabbed it, trying to pull her to him, but she resisted.

"This way."

The heat in his eyes was like a switch going off inside her. She was suddenly beautiful, powerful, and capable of taking what she wanted. And dammit, she wanted him. He wasn't the right decision for her future, because he'd never be interested in staying in her small town—in staying with her. But he was the right decision for today simply because she was tired of fighting how she felt about him, tired of dreaming about a happily ever after that might never come, and all along, she'd have missed out on some mighty fine happy for right nows.

But deep in her heart, she felt the kernel of hope bloom just from the look in his eyes. She felt the swelling of love in her chest at the sight of his need.

For her.

She was helpless against her internal romantic, the side that hoped for what couldn't be. The side that dreamed when she stared at the endless waves of the

Atlantic or ran her fingers along the hundred-year-old stone of the Fountain of Youth in Van Buren Square.

He needed her, and she wanted to be there for him until the time came when she had to say goodbye and watch him leave Cape Van Buren.

At least, with an ass like his, the watching would still be a pleasure.

She walked him back to her sanctuary. Her room was lush and bright in tones of white, and she'd never look at it the same way again. Pushing him back to the bed, she skimmed her eyes over his body. He was built like the foundation of the damn lighthouse out on the Cape—a broad chest and broader shoulders, supporting the weight of muscles that he'd fed and fed well, and all of the deliciousness tapered down to a V that boggled the mind and made her go dumb because, when she looked at the length of him waiting for her, all she wanted to do was scream "hellz yeah" and climb on up.

She grabbed a condom from a box under the open shelf of her nightstand, then ripped the foil open. While holding her lower lip between her teeth, she wrapped her hand around his thickness and rolled the condom all the way to the base.

He sucked in a breath, then held it. "Sage, if you don't hurry up and quit playing around with him, this is going to be over before you get to see my best work."

She raised a brow, then crawled over him to straddle his waist. Spreading her hands across his chest, she said, "I could have sworn I saw your best work back by the door."

"Woman, you haven't seen nothing yet."

He gripped her hips and slid her back and forth over his length.

She leaned down, then pressed her mouth to his and made demands with her tongue she had never known the language for—until today. With her eyes open, she kissed him, and his full lips curved, revealing a dimple in his cheek that made her want to give him everything he asked for. The intense blue of his eyes pulled her in as if nothing else existed outside of their heated bubble.

"You see me," he said.

She glanced down between them with intent. "All of you."

But he didn't smile, he studied her harder, his hands gripping her hips. "We won't have forever, Sage. You know I can't give you that."

On a nod, she quieted him with her lips. She didn't want to talk about what couldn't be; she wanted to feel everything that could.

Holding herself until she was poised at his round, smooth head, she lowered, taking him in, inch by inch. Spirals of pleasure poured out from her center, down the front of her thighs, and over the lower swell of her stomach.

"Goddammit, you feel too good," he gritted out. "I can't get you out of my mind."

He encouraged her to lean forward until he closed his hot mouth over her breast. A low groan of pure satisfaction floated to her ears, and her own joined his in the most sensual duet she'd ever heard. As she moved, hearts floated about her once again.

She tried to shake them off, but they stubbornly remained, and he felt so good she didn't care.

His movements slowed from sizzle to savor, and she followed, happy to eke out the experience as long as possible. Long strokes of skin on skin, fevered whispers, and promises that would be kept only at the moment.

His mouth was everywhere. "I want more. I need more." With hot hands, he grabbed fistfuls of her ass in a way that increased every sensation inside her and made her move faster once again. Tension coiled at her center, so tight that she pushed away from his chest until she was bowed backwards over his legs, moving on him without missing a beat.

He massaged her breasts with a gentle squeeze that she felt throughout her whole body, then he trailed the backs of his fingers down the center of her chest, down her stomach, until his thumb found that part of her that was like lighting the wick on a stick of dynamite.

A white-hot ball of energy burst throughout her body until every nerve ending shot off like a sparkler from Fourth of July.

"Parker," she grated out his name as contraction after contraction demanded she keep moving.

With one smooth push, he rolled her onto her back and threw her legs over his shoulders, then rode out her orgasm until falling over the edge into his own. His eyes squeezed shut, he pushed into her, demanding every last ounce of pleasure she had to give. His solid strokes slowed to easy ones, and their ragged breathing was the only sound left in the still of the night.

Falling to her side, he scooped her to him until his chest was against her back and the hairs of his thighs tickled the sensitive skin of her own. "What was that?" he asked, his arms wrapped around her, trembling in his aftershocks.

"That's what happens when you care." It was the wrong thing to say, but sometimes, the hard things were the right things.

He froze behind her, and there was a moment she almost wished she could take back the words. But only a moment, because the truth was, her heart had opened to him the day he'd saved her at Eclectic Finds Kataclysmic Kissing booth. "I think I'm falling for you."

Silence was her answer, then a slow exhale. "Then, grab onto something, Sage. Because that's a fall that will only end in you getting hurt."

Parker cussed like a sailor in his head, telling himself to quit acting like a jackass and tell Sage he had feelings, too. But he was terrified. She was one of the most generous women he'd ever met. She was passionate, intelligent, and sexy as hell. And her body did something to his he'd never felt before—and he'd felt a lot.

But Cape Van Buren was *her* home. And it was his grandfather's home. He couldn't imagine living day to day hoping to avoid the old man. Banon had made it clear Parker wasn't welcome, wasn't a part of this community. It was a rejection he'd rather not face again.

Not to mention, though he enjoyed the Cape and the in-your-face community, he missed the busy energy of New York City. and the mix of cultures and the anonymity it allowed that was so often a blessing.

In the end, the truth was…she deserved better.

It was the facts, but it hurt like hell. The idea of leaving town and not staring into her eyes as she talked about her Grandpa Horace, or not tasting her sweet lips whenever he was hungry for dessert, left him feeling hollow.

The board needed their answer. He could increase the paper's profit hand over fist, which would more than meet their needs and stabilize the infrastructure. By giving up the printing press, not to mention the decrease in overhead, and the rental income from turning portions of the building into offices, the paper would be able to keep Sage and hire five more cartoonists if they wanted to. Cape Van Buren was surprisingly tech savvy, even their more mature sector. With the right promotion to incentivize the readership and the increased ad space, sales would go through the roof. The *The Van Buren Tribune* would have a long and prosperous life.

At least he could give Sage that. Her grandfather's memory would be preserved. Maybe not the way she'd hoped, but in a way that would last.

With a measure of self-control, he hadn't known he possessed, he slid away from her. "I have to make a call."

She curled up in the comforter of her bed. "Sure."

Making his way through her apartment, he found his clothes, noticing all the touches that screamed Sage—the art on the walls, the heart-shaped pillows on her sofa, and the welcome mat that read, *creativity lives here.*

He threw on his briefs and slacks, then sat at her breakfast bar, moving the day's paper out of his way. Of course, it was open to the comic with Edward the gorilla and his lingerie.

"Mr. Edwards, yes, go ahead and schedule the board meeting. My initial assessment of taking the *Tribune* online still stands. After seeing what the town has to offer, I'm confident the news will translate as well, if not better, online. The change can happen immediately, I've been working on the system, and it's almost complete."

"How is Ms. Mathews taking it?"

Surprise skittered down Parker's back. The last thing he expected from his grandfather was compassion. For anyone.

Caught off guard, his chest tightened at the idea that his grandfather thought Parker and Sage were in a relationship. He down-played the situation to put any rumors to bed.

He cringed at the pun.

"Oh, she'll be fine. She can easily continue her comic online or take it elsewhere, if that's what she decides. That's the nice thing about hobbies. They're flexible."

"Parker, I think we need to talk," Banon said.

"I know...you want me out of town."

"No, I—"

"So, what time for the meeting?" he asked, cutting his grandfather off.

A heavy sigh floated over the connection.

Parker had no clue what else the man could say to drive his point home, but

61

he was no longer interested in hearing it.

After they settled the time for the board meeting, he set his phone aside, then scrubbed his hands through his hair. But the tension in the back of his neck wouldn't release, so he lifted his head and tried cracking his neck.

There, in the archway of her bedroom, was Sage—the bedsheets wrapped around her silky skin, her lips swollen from being kissed the right way, and eyes that shone with a mixture of betrayal and sadness.

Wait.

He pushed from the stool. "What happened?"

She swallowed hard. "You happened. A hobby? Did you really just call my life's work, a hobby?"

"Oh, shit. Sage, that's not how I meant it, it's just my grandfather—"

"Save it," she said, her voice trembling, making his chest squeeze hard around his lungs.

She pulled the sheets tighter about her, walked over to the sofa and picked up a pillow. "Get out of my apartment. I wouldn't want to bore you any longer with my hobby or my lame tendency toward love."

"I never said—"

She threw him a look, and it was a side of her he never wanted to see again— a combination of disgust and acceptance. "Please, you don't think I saw it on your face the day you walked into the *Tribune*? And every time since when I'd try and make you understand how integral this paper is to the homes of our community?"

A sick feeling twisted in his gut and seared through his spine. Even though he'd been talking a good game about leaving town and leaving Sage, being faced with the end was now an impossibility.

And he didn't know how he could fix it. "Listen, let's talk about this. I didn't mean anything by what I said. My grandfather caught me off guard, and I spoke without thinking."

"It's fine. Really."

Walking to the door, she shook her head, then opened it for him to leave. A warm, watery smile curved her lips. "Just go. It's clear now what the problem is."

With an ache spreading like wildfire across his chest, he grabbed his things. "What's that?"

"I see you, but you don't see me."

CHAPTER 9

*S*aturday morning, Sage rushed into her office at the *Tribune* and closed the door. Pressing her back against it, she pushed her fist against her mouth to muffle the sound of her tears. She'd fled from her apartment as soon as she'd heard the news about the paper through the Cape Van Buren current—it was faster than the Gulf Stream off the coast.

She couldn't stay where she could still see her rumpled bed sheets—she'd slept on her couch—where she could still smell the warm scent and feel the firm caress of the man who'd broken her heart.

But the newspaper wasn't much better. All her memories with her grandfather—reading the comics at the breakfast table, the two of them taking over the empty building after hours. All those magical moments were being stripped away like the waves do to the sands along the coast.

That thing that made her who she was, that bliss her grandfather had always encouraged her to find, the whole infrastructure of his support, was being ripped down like an out of date set of curtains over a kitchen sink—unimportant and unimpressive to everyone else, but priceless for the mother who had watched her kids play through that window while washing dishes and making years of memories.

She walked over to her desk, chewing on her lower lip. With a practiced hand, she laid out a fresh sheet of drawing paper.

The view and laughter of the firemen working through some drill below without their shirts on couldn't even ease her pain. For some reason, they all seemed somehow lacking.

What was the world coming to when she didn't find pleasure in ogling Van Buren's finest?

Because you just had the finest yesterday.

And she wasn't talking about Maxine's moonshine.

The letter she'd finally received from Andrews McMeel Publishing sat at the corner of her desk, and the sight of it made everything seem worse. She turned it upside down, then set her cup of drawing pencils on top of it.

Opening it would mean facing her dreams, and she wasn't ready. If it was good news—which wasn't likely—she wouldn't be able to enjoy it having lost her grandfather's paper. If it was bad news, well then, everything she loved would be lost to her all in the span of twenty-four hours.

And that wasn't a reality she could face at the moment.

Long strokes of her pencil served as an immediate salve, like a light wash of cleansing rain over her brain. Each stroke relieved a little more of her pain and replaced it with pleasure. That was the magic in drawing, in any kind of art, really. Its beauty was hers for the taking whenever she needed to take it.

A knock sounded at her door.

Pushing her hair behind her ears, she straightened in her chair. "Come in."

Banon James Edwards I poked his head around the corner of the door and cleared his throat. "I thought I heard you in here."

She swiveled to face him, surprised to see him standing there with his fine suit and polka dot tie—Evette's doing—it reminded Sage of the icing design on the North Cove Confectionary's Blueberry Lemon twist cupcake.

"May I come in?"

Asking for permission was unexpected, as well. It was like her whole damn world was being turned upside down.

A look of concern filled his blue eyes—eyes that reminded her of Parker and left her heart pumping empty. "So, you heard about the news," he said.

She nodded, not trusting her voice to speak.

"I know how much this place means to you. Horace used to spin tails to me of all his dreams for his little Hershey Kiss while we drank Scotch and smoked cigars like important men of men when we were young. We were such fools." His tone was wistful and formal and reminded her of everything she'd lost.

"At least, I was. Horace was one in a million of men. Do you know he stood as my best man at my wedding?"

She shook her head. Banon Edwards had never been one to share, and since she was young, she'd learned to stay away from his bark. She'd never asked her grandfather about him, just always thought their friendship was odd. Horace loved people. Banon loved himself.

At least, that's how it appeared to her, anyway.

"My grandson presented his findings to the board. He did a very thorough job going over the projections and giving the newspaper multiple options. The research and stats left no question as to the direction we need to take *The Van Buren Tribune*. I have to say, he delivered and then some, exceeding not only their expectations but my own. And that's no easy feat."

She swallowed. "Parker is a hard worker, sir. One of the best."

He studied her face. "You're hurt by his decision." His question seemed ridiculous to her, but his expression was open and curious.

"Devastated. I knew it was coming, but it seems so much worse..." She couldn't finish.

"Coming from the man you love."

Her eyes snapped to his.

Who was this man, and what had he done with Banon Edwards?

"I've learned a lot over the past week or so. Evette has opened my eyes to many things. My grandson, though he doesn't realize it, has opened my eyes to many more."

Sage studied the old man, her heart turning over at the look of regret in his eyes. She was happy he was finally seeing Parker for who he really was—a good, hard working, caring man who had simply been trying to carve his place within the family circle, instead of sitting outside and looking in.

"One of those being that I've been holding Parker responsible for the actions of his father for years. Let's just say that looking at Parker was a constant reminder of not being loved by my own son. It killed me, so I kept my grandson at a distance that hurt less. But in doing so, I hurt him a lot. I see that now."

Her heart turned over for the years of missed memories in the old man's eyes. "Evette's pretty special," she offered.

He cleared his throat in a gruff cough. "Don't hold Parker responsible for the decisions of the board. In the end, we're the ones who let the paper fall into this precarious position."

"I just think there should be another way. Grandpa Horace worked so hard, had such big dreams that included the families of Cape Van Buren."

Banon looked over the walls of her office, then past her shoulder to the fire station outside. "That he did. That he did." He turned his attention back to her. "Things change. It won't be the same, but I think if we try hard enough, we can continue to honor his direction."

He moved back to the door. "It might be too late for me when it comes to Parker, but it doesn't have to be for you."

She shook her head. "He doesn't get me, doesn't *see* me, Mr. Edwards. Not the real me."

"I think *all* he sees is you."

The door closed with a soft *snick* behind him.

Sage stared at it a moment, then turned back to her sketch. Parker's face stared up at her with intense blue eyes and a knowing smile. She could pretend not to care, but the truth was in her art.

Holding her breath, she pulled the envelope from the publisher out from under her pencil cup. Grandpa Horace always told her to go after her bliss. She loved Parker, but she couldn't make him love her, so it was time to be brave, and go after her other true love.

With fear in her heart and hope in her veins, she opened the envelope.

~

*P*arker pulled in a deep breath. His blood rushed in his ears, and his heart beat wildly in his chest. He hadn't felt this kind of panic since dinging his grandfather's car with a grocery cart back in high school—the car he shouldn't have been driving.

Shoving a hand through his hair, he knocked on Sage's door.

Silence.

He tried again. "Sage, let me in. Please."

Nothing.

The tension in his shoulders only worsened with each passing second.

Checking over his shoulder, he checked along the lush grounds of North Cove gardens to make sure no one called the police on his ass.

He couldn't leave Cape Van Buren with her thinking he didn't take her seriously. If anything, it was the very reason he was leaving. He took her happiness so seriously that he didn't want to be the one to screw it all up.

Wrapping his hand around the door handle, he turned it, expecting to find it locked, but the door opened, leaving him standing there, unsure about what to do next. "Sage?"

With a furtive glance over his shoulder one more time, he stepped inside.

The apartment was silent and smelled of strawberries and sugar cookies with hints of his cologne. It was a combination that should never work, but did, as if made for each other from the start. He shook his head.

Peeking in her room, he found the bed unmade, with the sheet she'd covered herself in on the floor as if she hadn't slept there since. The bathroom light was on, and her drawers left half opened. All signs pointed to her leaving in a rush, and a heaviness settled in his gut.

The door opposite her room was closed, and just to be sure, he knocked lightly. "Sage?" He turned the knob and pushed it open.

Her studio.

He should shut the door and walk away. The space was sacred to her; she cherished it and poured her whole heart into everything she did there. Respecting her wishes for privacy was important.

But then, his eyes lit on a sketch hanging from the opposite wall, and his feet propelled him forward all on their own.

He devoured sketch after sketch after sketch.

Having no idea didn't even begin to describe his ignorance.

Sage didn't just see inspiration and draw something. She felt it, then put that feeling on paper.

There was a sketch of Evette propositioning his grandfather at the festival. It wasn't just fear on the old man's face, but curiosity and, dare he say it, yearning? He didn't know if his grandfather was even capable of such emotions—but there they were.

Another captured the kids at the vineyard, peeking out from behind grape vines with delight and wonder on their faces.

He approached her drawing table.

Multiple sketches were tacked to the surface, his own eyes staring back at him. He was strong, capable, with kind eyes and a playful smile—much different than the damn gorilla named Edward.

He picked one up, the corners of his lips pulling into a grin. This one was of the two of them on the ground, a freaked-out Moby snorting off in the distance.

The look on his own face as he stared down at her in shock and awe was unmistakable.

Because it was the same feeling in his heart.

Love.

Goddammit.

He loved her.

She may not have known it, but it was in her sketches all the same. He might be scared of hurting her, scared of facing his grandfather's disappointment day after day if he stayed, but the love he had for Sage, as well as the love she had for him, was all around him, painting the room in floating hearts.

Hell, he hadn't even thought of Cape Van Buren as Tiny Town in days. Sage had wheedled her way in and set her hooks without him even guessing that was her intent, much less knowing.

Now, he just hoped it wasn't too late.

She loved him, but would she give him the chance to love her back?

Did he even deserve it?

It was time he grew a pair and found out.

And it was time he relinquished the hold Banon James Edward I had on him. If his grandfather didn't want him in his life, Parker would set him free. But if Sage didn't want him in hers, he didn't know what the hell he'd do.

Because suddenly, having to leave Cape Van Buren was no longer possible.

He couldn't live without a beating heart.

And his beat on the Cape.

～

Throwing open the board room door, Parker rushed in. "I'm sorry I'm late, but there's been a change of plans."

His grandfather pushed back from the table, and for the first time, Parker saw how old he was getting. "Parker..."

"Mr. Edwards, I know what you're going to say, but please, hear me out. This isn't just about the *The Van Buren Tribune*, but about the people, too."

His grandfather raised a brow with hope in his eyes. "People, you say?"

Parker had to look twice to make sure he was still talking to his grandfather and not someone he'd only mistaken to be him.

"Does this 'people' happen to be Sage Mathews?"

Rubbing the back of his head, Parker blinked. All of a sudden, it was as though he'd been pushed into a twilight zone. He looked from his grandfather to the board members gathered around the table and nodded.

Banon slapped his hands together. "Well, then close the door and sit down, boy. We've got work to do."

Parker shook his head, unable to process what was happening. "This will change the bottom line from my original assessment and recommendation, Grandfa...I mean—"

Banon raised a hand to stop him. "Grandfather is fine, but let's ease into it. It's been a while since I've been comfortable hearing it. I don't know what we can make of our relationship, or if you even want to try. But I'm telling you, I'd like the chance to find out. If we decide we still don't like each other, well then... we won't be the first Edwards to have a relationship in name only."

A weird feeling of weightlessness seemed to move Parker to take a seat. He was numb and cold and unsure of what to say. He'd faced nothing but judgement for years. Was he capable of something more with the man? He glanced at the board, but they sat at attention as if Banon's speech was an expected agenda item, and his grandfather stared back at him...waiting.

"I don't think this is the time—"

Banon nodded. "We'll take care of that later. Horace would have my head if he was here right now. We need to find a way to keep Ms. Mathews drawing that damned gorilla."

Parker nodded with a wide grin. "I have an idea, but I need the board's approval first."

"Well, let's have it, Mr. Edwards," his grandfather said. "You're the expert, and you know we only hire the best."

CHAPTER 10

*E*arly Sunday morning, Sage settled into her seat in The Cape Bistro's
outdoor seating cafe with her sketch pad, her pencils, and her newly
broken heart. The outdoor patio area was shaded by two arbors, that currently
sported hanging heaters, a few tables, and potted rose bushes as well as the
newspaper box shared with the Van Buren hotel. Well, that wouldn't be around
much longer—the box, not the hotel.

Parker had seen to that.

A removable wrought iron gate edged around the perimeter gave a distinct
impression of an eating space without blocking any views of the lush North
Cove Gardens with its artistic plant-scapes, brick pathways, and pond. But she
only stared at the blank page in front of her, frozen in the numbness of her loss,
the kind that made three days feel like three years and breathing an effort.

With all the buzz around her, she'd considered eating inside, but couldn't
stand the idea of being closed in. Holing up in her apartment hadn't been working, either. If Parker wasn't knocking on her door, asking to talk to her as she
hid tucked in the corner of her couch clutching her heart pillows, then she was
lying in her bed, holding the sheets to her nose, breathing in his cologne. Sleep
plagued her with dreams of him, but the day wasn't much better. That's what
happened when you fell in love with someone who couldn't love you back.

He'd wanted to apologize, but she couldn't bear to see him again and then have to watch him walk away. Because he would walk away. He'd already proven that he didn't really see her. All this time, he'd looked at her comics as a hobby instead of who she was when even to a blind person, it would have been so clear. Cape Van Buren and her views on the people were way too romantic for his jaded New York City heart.

It was what it was.

But that also meant she had to pull up her boot straps and walk ahead. She couldn't save her grandfather's paper, or their legacy of the comic he helped her start, but she now had a new and exciting opportunity to make him proud. So, she ignored Parker's calls, both on the phone and in person, and tried to put one foot in front of the other.

The last Sunday paper would run today, announcing the new big, bright change for the *The Van Buren Tribune*, so all she had to do was get through the day, and then, maybe tomorrow, she could figure out what exactly she was going to do with the rest of her life.

"Wow, you're really talented." Alora tapped the blank page, then pulled out a chair and dropped into it. She had that secret little grin on her face that told everyone that her current man of the hour, Adam, had launched her day off right—and possibly more than once.

A small twinge of jealousy melted with the yearning tiptoeing through Sage's chest. Maybe Cape Van Buren and its beautiful rocky shores weren't her answer to finding love. Either way, seeing Alora so happy made Sage really glad that it was for so many others.

She grunted. "I'm waiting for inspiration."

"That's not like you. You normally just take it. I've seen you burst into a drawing frenzy from a weed breaking through a crack in the sidewalk."

Suddenly, her blank sheet of paper was swiped from the table by a fuzzy muzzle.

"Hey!" She lunged to grab it back but thought better as Moby munched it into a ball then hawked it out onto the sidewalk like a spit ball.

Alora finished tying off his rope to the wooden post of the gate. "If you can't beat 'em..." She pulled out a chair, laughing at Sage. "That's what he thinks of your blank page," she said, sitting down.

Sage ran her gaze over Alora's buttery complexion. "What are you doing here? And why did you bring Moby? He's a menace."

Alora quickly reached to cover the young moose's ears. "Don't talk about him like that. He's sensitive. I'm looking after him for Grandie Evette." Turning to Moby, she rubbed his nose and offered him an apple. "Forget what the mean old lady said, boy. She's just grumpy because she's about to go through another dry spell."

Throwing her hands up, she made a face, then grabbed another sheet of paper from her bag. "You know what? You two can go suck it somewhere else."

"Ooooh!" Alora crooned. "Maxine and Grandie would be wicked proud of you for that one."

Sage looked around the patio with a shake of her head. "Speak of the devil and his possie."

Maxine and Judge Carter were walking up with Evette and Banon Edwards. Now there was a love match she'd never expected, but the smile on the old man's face proved the magic of it all—his smile even resembled one of joy versus strain this morning. Grandie winked at her as they took a seat at another table. She wiggled her fingers in return, then turned back to her cousin.

"What in the heck is going on here? The Cape Bistro patio is never this busy on a Sunday morning. Everyone's usually nursing one of ShellyAnne's magic brews from the Flat Iron Coffeehouse and walking in the park.

The newspapers disappeared one by one from the box, and she nudged Alora, who was whispering to Moby. "They're all in for a big surprise. That's the last print newspaper for Cape Van Buren. We'll see just how much everyone loves it a month from now when the family's noses are in their phones at the breakfast table instead of scouring through the paper together, making plans for the weekend." She crossed her arms and sat back, feeling a little raw by the buzz of excitement.

Apparently, she'd been way off.

The people of Cape Van Buren not only didn't seem to mind the announcement of the change, but by the sound of their laughter, they loved it.

Memory bubbles of her grandfather popped about her head as a heavy weight settled in her belly. All this time, she really believed her comics had made a difference, that the paper had really brought the town together.

A fool didn't even come close to how she felt.

Pressing her lips together, she tried to ignore the jovial chatter and focus on the drawing paper in front of her, but all she saw before her was nothingness.

And to think, she'd moved here with the idea that little seaside town of Cape Van Buren held her answers to everything.

Evette's laughter caught her attention, and she threw a glare four tables over.

"Wow, someone sure is grouchy this morning," Alora noted.

Sage cringed. "I'm sorry. I just..."

Her friend took a big bite of a double-dipped chocolate eclair while trying to dodge Moby's muzzle. "Just what?"

Sage looked back and forth between her cousin and the moose. Things may not have ended up as her perfect happy ending, but she was surrounded by family, and she was getting published in the same house as *The Far Side*. The reality of it all hit her hard.

"I was going to say, I thought the paper meant more to the community, that Grandpa Horace meant more, but you're here. Without even being asked, you're all here with me."

The two women grinned. "Of course, we are."

This time, Maxine's satisfied chuckle met Sage's ears.

"What in the heck? That's it..." She shoved up from the table. "I want to know what they think is so darned funny."

Alora pressed her lips together, but delight shone from her eyes. The kind of delight fueled by possibility and promises.

Marching over to the paper box, she inserted her money, then yanked down the door. Grabbing the paper, she shook it open and scanned through the pages. A sudden hush fell over the crowd as she turned to the last page.

The comics.

"I don't understand." She shook her head. There, in the place where her comic was usually displayed...was a comic.

But she hadn't submitted one.

The colors were the same, and Edward the gorilla was almost the same, but something was different. The title read, *Even Big Dumb Animals Need a Second Chance.* Edward was on his knees with a pleading grin, begging at the feet of a young woman with familiar chocolate brown eyes and matching hair.

The woman was reading the *Tribunel*, which boasted the headline, *Tribnue to Keep Sunday Print.* And in one of the gorilla's hands was a group of red heart balloons that floated above their heads.

73

Tears stung her lids as hope flared in her chest. With a shake of her head, she turned back toward Alora and the two couples. "What does this mean?"

And there before her, on his knees, was Parker, holding a bunch of red heart balloons. Balloons printed with *I love you*.

"I made a mistake," he said with nerves in his voice that she'd never heard before. "I came here ready to hightail it back to New York as soon as I arrived, but I'd never counted on falling for a romantic cartoonist who would challenge my very livelihood."

His bright blue eyes pleaded with her to understand. "I said the wrong thing. A stupid thing. More than once, actually."

She grabbed his hands. "Get up."

The crowd sucked in a breath, and Evette mewed in delight.

"You love New York. You aren't looking for forever in Tiny Town."

Parker cupped her face. "I am a big, dumb animal, remember? I was so focused on proving myself to my grandfather..."

They both looked at Banon who winced and gave a small nod of his head.

"Focused on saving the paper and proving that I was the best that missed what you kept trying to tell me all along. This paper brings the town together. Just look around us."

For the first time, she really studied everyone sitting around the The Cape Bistro. Alora, Evette and Banon, Maxine and Judge Carter, Ryker and Larkin with Blayne and Jay, and even Moby were all there. And so many, many more.

They were all there because of the paper.

"But this is the last one." She held the newsprint to her chest and sniffed.

Brushing a tear from her cheek with his thumb, he grinned. "The *The Van Buren Tribune* is going digital."

Her shoulders sagged.

He continued, "Monday through Saturday. But the Sunday paper will be beefed up and remain in print so it can continue to unite this community just the way your grandpa Horace had intended. Besides, you can clearly tell from the comic, I've fallen for you, too. There are hearts literally floating above my head."

Sage glanced up and grinned. She was afraid to speak, afraid to move, afraid it was all a dream. Love for Parker and her coastal paradise in Cape Van Buren washed over her, and she had to grab onto him to steady herself.

"I've been so miserable. You tried to call, and you stopped by, but Cape Van Buren...I..."

She closed her eyes to compose herself. "I wasn't what you wanted. You wanted New York and probably someone with more designer on her sleeve than emotion."

He shook his head, then pressed his lips to hers. A warm sensation of acceptance filled her heart and chest. "I want you, Sage. I want the way you see the world, the way you hope, the way you believe in the good and the happily ever afters. I was just too afraid to admit it, to disappoint you as I thought I had my grandfather."

"And my art?"

"I'm sorry for what I said. I was a complete ass and clearly had no idea what I was talking about. Your art is brilliant." He looked a bit sheepish. "I saw your studio."

Her jaw dropped open as she tried to imagine him in her space, filling it up with his broad shoulders and chiseled jaw.

"I know. I'm sorry, but I'd gone back to talk to you, and you weren't home, but the door wasn't locked. It's amazing, Sage. You...are amazing. *The Van Buren Tribune* needs the smiles you put on their faces every Sunday."

Her heart turned over in her chest. "Even if the headliner is a gorilla named Edward?"

Parker kissed her again, and she sunk into it, ignoring the tittering "oohs" and "ahhs" all around her. "Especially with the gorilla, Edward. If things are going the way I hope they are, then he's turned out to be the best wingman I've ever had."

She wrapped her arms and heart around the man who had found his way inside and made her dreams about Cape Van Buren come true. She winked. "We need to talk about a raise. The paper's cartoonist has her own book coming out."

"Sage, that's amazing!" He picked her off her feet and squeezed. "What's it called?"

With her feet once again on solid ground—though, truth be told, she still felt like she was floating—she gave him a saucy grin. "Drawing You In. It's about this gorilla..."

She didn't get to finish her story because Parker silenced her with a kiss that would surely make it into next Sunday's paper.

And with her friends and family all around her, celebrating the special blend of love that could only be found on the Cape, Sage's own happily ever after had begun.

~

Did you love *Draw You In?* Reviews make a huge difference to an author's career. I would be extremely grateful if you are able to take a few seconds and leave a review on your favorite retailer!

Don't forget to join my mailing list for your **FREE** copy of *Honor on the Cape,* and for new release alerts, a monthly self-exam reminder, and NO spam! Visit my website to sign-up!

~

ALSO AVAILABLE IN THE ON THE CAPE SERIES
Love on the Cape
Honor on the Cape
Cherish on the Cape
Draw You In
One Jingle or Two
Love, Honor & Cherish: The On the Cape Trilogy

ACKNOWLEDGMENTS

To my children and husband, otherwise known as my heart and soul, thank you for believing in me and always knowing I could do this even when I didn't. I love you. To my big brothers, Tommy, Todd, and Billy—as goofy as I am, you've always held me up. To Paula, my sister of the heart, I'm forever in awe of you. And to my mom, who's continued to mother me from the other side, I hope I have a fraction of your grace. Thank you.

It's a lovely feeling to know I'm not alone in this dream of mine. Thank you to my editor, Jessica Snyder, my copy editor, Jennifer Wiers Serevino at Twitching Pen. Thank you, Jessica Snyder and Julia Pierce for your eagle eyes while proofing this story. Thank you to the Romantics, your love lifts me up, and to my street team, MK & CO, for your friendship and for believing in me. I love everyone in this family, from the very first to the still-to-come.

Thank you to Marina Adair, my dear friend and talented romance writer. This book was originally inspired to take part in her St. Helena Vineyards. I'm so happy to be able to bring it to the Cape.

One more exuberant thank you to the readers of this book. Experiencing life with you in this way is magical. I hope that at least one scene, one line, or simply one word resonates with each of you. And to my sisters and brothers in the fight against breast and all types of cancer. I know both sides, having lost my mom to breast cancer at a young age, and having survived cancer myself. My writing is one of the things that carries me through. I have many more books to write.

Thank you. Hugs, loves, and peanut butter,

MK

ABOUT THE AUTHOR

MK Meredith writes contemporary romance promising an emotional ride on heated sheets. She believes the best route to success is to never stop learning. Her lifelong love affair with peanut butter continues, and only two things come close in the battle for her affections: gorgeous heels and maybe Gerard Butler...or was it David Gandy? Who is she kidding? Her true loves are her husband and two children who have survived her SEAs (spontaneous explosions of affection) and lived to tell the tale. The Merediths live in the DC area with their large fur baby...until the next adventure calls.

www.mkmeredith.com

mk@mkmeredith.com

facebook.com/mkmkmeredith

twitter.com/mkmkmeredith

instagram.com/mkmkmeredith

bookbub.com/authors/mk-meredith

amazon.com/author/mk-meredith

ALSO BY MK MEREDITH

THE ON THE CAPE SERIES

Love on the Cape

Honor on the Cape

Cherish on the Cape

Draw You In

One Jingle or Two

Love, Honor & Cherish: The On the Cape Trilogy

THE SCRIPTED FOR LOVE SERIES

There's no place like paradise and the happy ever afters found in the film industry of Malibu, CA.

Love Under the Hot Lights

Just a Little Camera Shy

A Heated Touch of Action

THE INTERNATIONAL TEMPTATION SERIES

A strong dose of decadence along with a side of tall, dark, and sexy in your favorite travel destinations.

Playing the Spanish Billionaire

Seducing the Italian Tycoon

THE SEATTLE CRUSH SERIES

Seducing Seven

STANDALONE TITLES

Not Your Usual Boob: The Good, Bad, and Wonky of Breast Cancer